Wash Us and Comb Us

By Barbara Deming:

PRISON NOTES (*1966*)

RUNNING AWAY FROM MYSELF:
A Dream Portrait of America Drawn from
the Movies of the Forties (*1969*)

REVOLUTION & EQUILIBRIUM (*1971*)

WASH US

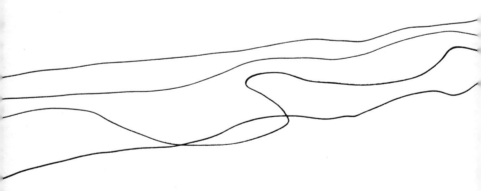

Drawings by Jane Watrous

AND COMB US

stories by Barbara Deming

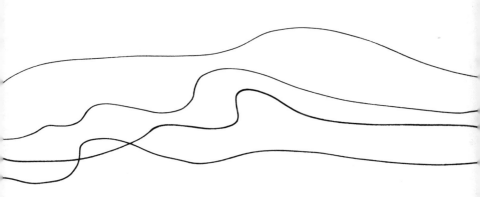

Grossman Publishers   New York   1972

ACKNOWLEDGMENTS
"Death and the Old Woman" originally appeared in *Charm* (November 1954) under the title "The Siege," "An Invitation" originally appeared in *The New Yorker* (August 8, 1953) under the title "A Giro."

for Madou

CONTENTS

Wash Us and Comb Us

She wrote to her husband, "You can be proud of me. I speak to nobody. I cut even the dog here, who would like to walk me to the beach, but I do as you say—I keep to myself." This letter was dated Tuesday. Saturday she wrote, "What a strange household! They never get out in the sun. The beach is a little bit of a walk, so they just don't go. Yesterday they put on suits and played the hose on each other out in the yard!" Her husband smiled to himself. "Now it begins," he thought. "But she has had at least this week in which to shed her skin, there by herself in the sun." He could see her plainly, standing upstairs in her room ("I've changed rooms. That damned palm tree kept me awake, knocking at the glass. I kept sitting up in bed calling out 'Just a moment!' They probably think I'm out of my head")—he could see her by her window, which looked out now on the front yard ("The mother-in-law takes the child out sometimes for a little turn, as though he were the dog")—standing not squarely before it but at its edge, her hand on the net curtain to draw it aside —rapt suddenly, freezing in that posture as an animal will when it scents upon the wind something new to it—her hand very lightly touching the net, for she half pretends to herself that she does not stand there, peering out. For all its concentration, there is about her posture a hesitant, a shy air. ("If I painted," he had often told her, "I would paint you just like that, Nina." "Just like what?" she would always ask.) Or she stands, he mused, out on the road, returning from the beach or from her walk into town at meal time—at a little distance from the house stopping short, as the wind carries to her some curious fragment of their speech, and she tenses, like a dog pointing. "And it isn't polite to point," he was used to teasing her. ("If you find it uncomfortable to be with me," she would begin, "why—" "I never have cared for ease," he would tell her. "I choose to live with you.")

His visions of Nina were accurate. Those first days she did as he said. ("Get quiet in yourself. The reviews missed the point. Put that behind you. Last week a patient died whom I should have known

3

how to save. I could mourn him and let all my other patients fade away. Get back to work again. But first get quiet in yourself. Try not to get involved down there with other people.") She wrote him, "You are always right." Away from him, she granted him much, though, bound by her nature, she was unable to do so when they stood face to face. It was good for them both to have her go away now and then. Those first days she spoke to no one. "She's a peculiar woman, this new roomer of yours," the mother-in-law, Mrs. Bruce, remarked to Cathy, her daughter, and Andy, her daughter's husband. "She smiles and then runs." Nina would stand up in her room waiting for the moment when she could descend without being seen; she would listen until voices, footsteps dispersed, and then hurry down the stairs and out and start off for beach or town walking very fast, her eyes straight ahead of her, primly, as if in blinders. The dog gave her trouble. He was a poodle, with a poodle's delight in confusion, and as he heard her leave her room, he'd place himself on the bottom stair and turn over on his back, his paws in the air. Sometimes she couldn't make him budge and she'd have to climb over him. "Poor pup," she wrote. "He's bored here, I think, and he'd like to latch onto me for a little fun. But I'm very strict. I cut him dead." She stayed at the beach most of the day. Setting out with picnic lunch and a big blanket to spread, she found herself a spot between sand dunes where few people strayed and from which she could spy out any invaders well in advance, and she stared up into the Florida sun and stared out into the shining Gulf—a small defiant figure, barricaded upon the sand. As she burned there, and as she immersed in that sea, she began to glance about her a little less suspiciously; her face began to smooth, her motions to soften. She wrote, "When I return, I think maybe I'll be possible to live with again. You were right that I should come down here. You are always right." And she began to get to work—putting in a couple of concentrated hours before she set out each morning.

But after about a week—as her husband had anticipated—it began. It was first of all the child she couldn't ignore. "The kid cries in his sleep," she wrote. "It's uncanny. They go rushing down the hall to him. It's a listless daytime household, but he shakes them up at night. Or maybe that's why they *are* so sleepy all day long. But children are uncanny. He doesn't know it but he's trying to cry them into their senses. What do they think they're doing down here? It's the mother-in-law's house, really, even if they think they're running it. Fuller is a painter, it turns out. But he never never goes outside. Non-objective, you see, so what does it matter? He paints mostly in the evening, by electric light. When the little boy can't get at his paints, he explains. Well really! As it is, the little boy gets at nothing at all." She began to woo the child. She'd spot him in the corner of the yard, or hovering in the parlor, and beckon him to her, then close his fist on a bag of sweets she'd found in town, wink at him and abruptly head on up to her room. One day she met him out on the road, walking with Mrs. Bruce, and she turned to walk along with them. She made the child a hat out of palm fronds. He got the giggles. "He wasn't used to such fun. And I gather Cathy Fuller thinks of herself as a photographer," she wrote. "But she never goes out of the house, either. There's lots of photographic equipment about, but all disassembled, the bits of it up on shelves everywhere, out of reach, again, of Ricky. Always poor Ricky. Between Ricky and the tourists! Because they're always pid-dling around the house supposedly fixing it up for the tourists. (I and a young college friend of theirs, Miles Richardson, we're the tourists as of now.) There's never much of a difference to be seen, I must say. They made a great fuss all one day about planting a little fruit tree on the lawn. Now every morning they rush out and water it, all of them together. Or they fret and fume at the typewriter together over ads for the place. Meanwhile, I gathered from Mady when she was talk-ing me into this place, they're down here to pursue their careers in freedom—away from the necessity of holding office jobs in New York. If they were having fun, it would be one thing. But they always seem so harrassed. I don't know, maybe they're not eating enough. I wouldn't be surprised if they were trying to save money that way and they're simply undernourished. They yawn all the time. I can't stand that look."

Nevertheless she remembered his words and her entrance into their lives was, for a little while still, in brief sallies only, retreats as sudden. On her way home from the beach one day, she spied Cathy in the kitchen, hunched over a pot—a slight girl with thin cheeks, with shining blue eyes. Ricky was hanging to her skirt—a thin shiny-eyed little boy, her image.

"No, don't, please, don't, don't," she was telling the boy.

"I *do,* Mommie," he replied, plaintive and stubborn.

Outside, the day was bright and there were quail on the lawn, wandered in from the semi-wilderness across the way. But the kitchen was sunless. The brown downfallen feathers of the palm tree shut out light at the window, and Cathy had the back door closed. She was peeling potatoes, slowly and drudgingly. The potatoes were a little old and full of blemishes, and she was scraping out each blemish painstakingly. She held the potatoes up close to her eyes, there in the dim room.

Nina darted in to her: "The sun is shining! There are funny birds at the corner of the lawn! Here, you mustn't sit in here! Come—let me show you!" And she gathered up the potatoes, cried to Rick, "You carry the pot!"—Cathy dazedly gathering up the peelings in a newspaper and following, out the back door into the sun, blinking. "Here! Here!"—Nina spread out the things on the stoop. "Sit here, no, here, where the sun has made it warm"—tugging at Cathy. "Put the bowl here! Now—and you can *see!* Sit comfortably, put your legs out, lean back against the wall. You take the joy out of life! Look, Ricky, at the birds. Creep very quietly and see how close you can get to one!" And then she was off, turning only to smile back at Cathy a vivid inquiring smile: "All right?"

But it was the Fullers' friend, Miles, who caused Nina to abandon once and for all this precarious solitude. Her husband could tell from her letters that *this* would be. She wrote, "There's a young man here who's not like the others. He has it like a fever—life. But yes, like a fever, because he is sick with it, I think. What is the matter with this generation? They are all of them afraid of their lives." She wrote, "He's a sculptor. They give him the shed to work in. He, for one, keeps at it, works half the day, in deadly earnest. . . . He has a noisy little car and wakes the household with it. An early dip? And then he's back in the yard. . . . A handsome boy. Yellow hair, black brows. Though it's an odd face—pinched somehow, and childish still. . . . I see him on the beach sometimes, but we skirt each other carefully. He eats with the Fullers often and he plays with the child sometimes, but mostly he keeps to himself. He sneaks out one door while I sneak out the other."

Miles, of course, had been watching Nina, too—as they all had in that household. One could not help but take notice of Nina. Even the rhythm of her typewriter could be distinguished from the rhythm of any other. The first time that Miles heard it—as he was about to leave the house one morning—he stopped at the door, straightening up as if roused out of sleep. It came in a sudden clatter, like rain bursting upon a tin roof—a storm that, after an interval during which he just stood there, his hand upon the door knob, as suddenly ceased. It was a strange music in this household. He began to watch her, at long distance—planted out there on the beach behind her improvised ramparts—or headed home, lugging her basket of provisions against the day, not content to take the winding shell road but cutting home directly through switch grass and bramble and palmetto, thrusting through, wearily those first days, angrily, but with an energy even then that startled him: a small woman, both hardy and delicate of frame—a little plump at the waist, but trim in spite of it, and vivid in all her motions. And her face was sculptured in such intensity, it brought to mind a figurehead dashed by the waters, outthrust in every sea. They talked of her at the house. And Cathy related the tale of Nina's sudden descent upon her in the kitchen. Miles was touched by the account.

Nina watched Miles and he watched her. But they carefully kept each his distance, exchanged nods, smiles, in passing, but—until one evening—nothing more. That evening, Nina was on her way home from dinner in town when from the roadway she glimpsed the family through the yellow square of parlor window, caught up in postures so odd, even for them—attitudes so becalmed—that she stopped, pursing her brows. She could see one of them sitting and one of them standing, each with hands out stiffly before him, unmoving. Once in the house, she turned from her accustomed path straight up the stairs, and went down the hall and looked into the parlor. The entire family was gathered. Miles was with them, too. He was reading Rick the fairy tale of "The Three Heads of the Well." His voice reached her while she was still in the hallway: " '. . . So she came to the well, on the brink of which she sat down, and no sooner had she done so than a golden head without any body came up through the water, singing as it came:

> " 'Wash me and comb me, lay me on the bank to dry
> Softly and prettily, to watch the passers-by.' "

"Well!" she exclaimed, "I thought *you* were all bewitched!"

They turned round to her. On a table was a heap of china, a dinner set—in fragments. In the midst of the fragments stood a large bottle of household cement. They sat there, each with a patched-together platter or plate or cup cradled in his hands, patiently holding the thing together in one piece, hands out, waiting for the glue to set. The dog was slumped in the center of the room rolling his eyes sadly from one of them to the other.

"My goodness!" said Nina.

Cathy's mother began to chatter explanations—a slight woman, like her daughter, but less frail, "all gristle," Nina had written to her husband. As Mrs. Bruce talked, her teacup came apart again in her hands. "When I went North after my husband's death, all the family china was stored in the shed. Oh dear, I moved! But the men packed it so clumsily that very nearly every piece is cracked. They were my grandmother's . . ."

"Lovely," murmured Nina.

The china was in a rose pattern. This made it easier to match the fragments, the mother chattered on.

"It's great training for something or other," said her son-in-law sleepily. He was a large good-looking youth with heavy rather slack-jointed limbs and a way of sitting as though he were resting a cumbersome burden.

Rick looked up. "Ricky will break them again," he said.

"No, Ricky will not," Cathy pronounced quickly, then flushed.

"But—maybe," said Rick lightly.

Nina glanced at Miles. "Why aren't *you* at work?" she asked.

"I'm lazy," he answered.

He sees it too, she thought—how outlandish this is—and so he doesn't help. Then, suddenly, he cast her a look. She withdrew her eyes, because the look sought her out.

"Miles will read some more?" Rick tapped at his arm. So Miles took up the story again:

> " '*Wash me and comb me, lay me on the bank to dry*
> *Softly and prettily, to watch the passers-by.*'

" ' "Certainly," she said, pulling out her silver comb.' "
Rick echoed, "Certainly."

The next day, Miles picked up Nina on the road. She had headed home a little early—restless, knowing really what was to come. It would be hard to say whether she was walking home to meet it or to avoid it. He drove up alongside her.

"Miss Wolf, may I take you anywhere?"

"Nina," she told him. "Fine," she said, "take me anywhere. Where were *you* going?"

He hesitated.

"I know," she said. "You were lying in wait for me."

They drove along in silence for a mile or so, she suddenly grave. "Well," she said, "how does the dinner set progress?"

He laughed.

"How long have you been down here?" she asked him.

Almost a month, he told her. Andy had written that they were running this place just—.

"And what in the devil do they think they are doing?" she demanded. "What were you reading last night? 'Sleeping Beauty'? There's your sleeping household! She's quite a woman, that Mrs. Bruce."

He began to explain the Fullers to her, as the friend who had told her about this place had explained them. Back in New York they'd have to take drudging jobs.

She exploded: "Well they'd be better off up there! It would be the real world, at any rate. Sitting around down here piecing this poor woman's life back together again for her! It's ridiculous!"

He laughed again. He said, "Well, they figure that fancy china will be an asset to them with the tourists. They're going to start serving dinner."

"Pooh!" she said. "A five and dime set would do just as well. Just let them give them enough to eat. Have they *had* any tourists to speak of?"

"Oh yes," he said, "they come and go. They're always rather pleased to see them *go*, of course."

"I can imagine," she said. "Ridiculous. Sitting around with the pastepot! Children should never live with their parents," she snapped. "And I know," she told him, as he turned to look at her; "I have a daughter."

"Doesn't she live with you?" he asked.

"Yes, she does," she told him. "And she shows it."

"And have you told her she'd do well to leave?" he challenged.

She told him, "Parents can't do that. A child has to pack up and

get out for himself—for his dear life."

Miles was silent. She looked sidewise at him and saw his eyes dull over, in a dreaming stare. She glanced away and sat quiet. She was suddenly like a school girl, with her hands in her lap, too shy to look at the boy who is asking her for the next dance.

They had passed the house now and turned left on the highroad that headed north out of town. The Fullers' house lay adrift at the very edge of town, down a meandering shell road that led from the highroad to the ocean. It had had this road to itself until a few years back, but now several tourist cottages edged in close. The town of Fiddler had been a fishing village, and could just still be called that, but the tourists and those who lived by them were beginning to claim it. Many of the younger fishermen had moved down shore to Sweetland: "Fish are wild things. They can't take the traffic." But a few of the old-timers were still to be seen there, moving among the tourists with a lordly disregard, as though they didn't even see them—the Yankees lined up along the sea wall with their poles out. ("The man who named the place must have had a vision. They look like a bunch of fiddler crabs on a spring day, their claws up in the air.") The village was set on a narrow spit of land, pointed south. Bay water lay on one side of it, and Gulf on the other. On the bay side were the wharves and on the Gulf side the new hotels were staking out the beach between them. Up by the Fullers', though, the beach still curved away under no eye but that of an occasional bungalow. The road out of Fiddler ran north on up toward St. Petersburg; it also doubled south around the bay to Sweetland, Royal City and the Tamiami Trail.

Miles drove fast. They sped along the sun-dazzled highway, flanked by its watery ditch—formed when the trail was thrown up out of the swamp. The top was down. Above them, up toward the sun, three buzzards floated like paper—turning in the fiery air like ashes stirred.

A billboard flashed at them: TURN BACK TO ROYAL CITY!—FUN! FUN! FUN!—CARNIVAL!

"Fun!" she exploded—"that's what they have none of. Living down here and they might as well be living in Hohokus. Puttering about—half-hearted!"

Miles stepped on the brake suddenly and swung left over a dilapidated wooden bridge onto a sandy road. A shack alongside it was falling in upon itself. Under the bridge, an ibis stood on one leg, hunched, silent, like a troll. "Ah yes," Miles said, "let there be fun."

She looked at him.

"I agree with you," he told her, "of course."

The car bounced high over the road. The way began to twist and grow sandier. At a sudden turn, the Gulf stretched out before them, sun-struck, grey under gold. Miles stopped the car. To their left ran a small inlet. A heron was fishing in it, lifting up his stalky fine-jointed legs, slow-motion, to wade the shallow water—motionless for moments as a painted bird; then, delicate and murderous, striking with long beak. Beyond, above the Gulf, a chorus of gulls was screaming, throats open, tongues showing. The waves hissed, casting up small shells, casting up driftwood, casting up somebody's torn swimming cap, little ruffled daisies adorning it. Again Nina glanced sidewise at Miles, and again she looked away. He squinted at this scene, scowling, as if he were confronted with hieroglyphics he must read. His face was suddenly all stress, all points: his brows drawn together, dipping; his cheeks pulled in.

She straightened up in her seat.

"What? Where to?" he asked her. "Is there some place you've wanted to see?"

"Maybe it had better be some other time," she said.

He swung the car round. They jolted back toward the main road, she sitting very quiet, her basket on her lap.

"How long will you be here?" she asked him.

He was not sure, he said. Another month at least. And she?

She was not sure, either, she said. She added, "I *must* get to work."

Back at the house, Andy and Rick were out on the lawn. Andy had his shirt off. It was draped over the little fruit tree. He had been raking the shell path to the front door and stood now, leaning on the rake, staring up at the house, musing—a big awkward frame house, painted yellow, with a shingle roof stippled yellow and green. A thin trumpet vine clung to one corner of the house as if undecided whether or not to climb. Rick was trying to borrow the rake, but his father wanted it for a prop.

As Miles turned the car in at the drive, Nina suddenly reached over and banged on the horn. Andy and Rick swung round. "Listen!" she called. "Go get your wife! We're all going to the carnival! Hurry up!"

"We are?" asked Miles, but she didn't look at him.

Andy strolled toward her, drawling, "Carnival?"

"Hurry up!" she called. "Go put your shirt on and get your wife!"

"She's doing laundry, I think," he mumbled.

"Tell her to stop," she said. "Come on, it's a holiday!"

"Holler day!" said the child.

"Yes, holler!" she told him. "Come on, jump in. You keep honking the horn till they're ready."

Rick clambered in and began to hit the horn with pleasure. Andy strolled off down the path, ducking his head. Mrs. Bruce appeared at an upstairs window: "Gracious, what is it?"

"It's just us, Mrs. Bruce," Nina called. "We're running off with your family for an hour or so."

Royal City was a boom town that had failed. Its brief main street contained a movie palace, the winter quarters of a small northern military academy, with a parade ground flanking it, two oversize hotels competing grimly for the patronage of visiting parents, a few shops and a very noisy bowling alley where, one gathered, the ambitions of the townsfolk now chiefly expended themselves. Off this street radiated several boulevards, lined by royal palms and sweeping past empty lots. Street lamps lit the vacant air. In one of these lots a bulldozer still squatted, next the great pile of brush it had gathered up, chewinks and sparrows alighting upon it to flick into the brush after seeds. In another, the carnival was pitched. The boy soldiers from the Academy were attending in numbers—soft little fellows, slope-shouldered, pudgy, belted into their soldierly uniforms, but here abandoning with relief the postures of the soldier. They trotted from

booth to booth, casting occasional nervous glances at their strolling mentors; they circled and circled on the merry-go-round. As Nina approached with her party, a mentor was ordering two to dismount; they had circled long enough. Nina flung at them, "Call a rebellion!" and the two stared at her, owl-eyed. Miles laughed loudly. He seemed in a state of nervous excitement and kept glancing round at Nina continually. But she always looked at someone else.

The merry-go-round was antique and circled rather slowly. "Come on!" Nina shouted to the man in charge, "make it go faster for us!"

"Faster faster!" one of the little soldiers took up her cry.

Another, on the sidelines, fanning himself with a long palm frond, leapt at the first soldier's steed, striking it on the flanks. "Get up!"

Andy was riding a little ahead of Nina, slouched in his saddle, long legs dangling, and she saw him yawn and stretch himself, staring up at the painted scenes the horses circled: a chalet in the snow, two squawking parrots. "Hey," she shouted to the boy, "Give that man's horse a smack! He's holding up the rest!" The boy squealed with laughter and darted in.

Andy pulled in his heels. "Who's riding this horse?"

She hooted, "Ride it, then!"

Cathy was laughing.

Miles watched with a curious smile disturbing his lips. He seemed almost in a trance.

They strolled among the booths. At each, Nina bought chances for all. "Come on! We're having fun!" At the shooting gallery, Miles made a hit and won a small pink straw hat.

"What I have always wanted," he said and perched it upon his head.

"My dear," Andy told him, "it's *you*."

"Do you think so?" asked Miles. Then he caught Nina's eye suddenly and he blushed.

Rick plucked at his sleeve. "Off silly hat!" Miles took off the hat and walked, swinging it in his hand, self conscious.

As they wandered at last toward the car, Andy and Miles, striding ahead of the others, halted at the fortune teller's booth. The woman sat behind a curtain but a large poster portrait eyed them boldly. SYBIL THE GYPSY SEE-ER, the lettering ran. "She looks a little like Nina," said Miles. There was a likeness—the eyes set in ambush deep under the brow, glancing forth, the delicately arched nose appearing to sniff the air.

Nina and Cathy and Rick came up to them. "We think she looks like you, Nina," said Andy, pointing.

"Certainly," she said. "We're sisters."

"So it's a gypsy you are," Andy teased.

"Certainly," she answered. "By trade." She spoke almost curtly.

"It's what any writer tries to do, isn't it? If he's any good. Tell fortunes. Any artist."

"A painter?" asked Andy.

She eyed him. "He must look behind life."

Andy gave a mock shudder.

"You may well shake," she told him. "I don't mean look for simple geometry."

On the way home, Nina was silent, and when they reached the crossroads outside of Fiddler, she asked to be dropped off at the café where she was in the habit of eating. They protested: she must eat with them. But she said no, another time; and she was curiously vehement. So they did as she asked. But Miles, when he had brought the others home, turned the car round again and announced that he was going to go back and join her.

Nina's café was the Paradise Café. It faced the main wharf—a small dilapidated building with a bright new sign: each letter in PARADISE another color. Inside, starfish painted blue adorned one wall. A large jukebox provided the chief source of light. There were five or six small tables, one waitress.

Nina didn't see Miles come in, and he stopped at the door, suddenly uncertain whether or not to join her. The place was almost empty. It was early still. The jukebox was silent. Two shrimp fishermen were having a beer and the waitress had sat down with them to visit for a moment. Nina was sitting by herself at a corner table, waiting for her dinner—her elbow on the table and her cheek resting upon her hand. She looked sad. She was withdrawn upon herself so utterly, he felt as one would feel who came, while tramping in the woods, upon a hermit's hut, the hermit sitting at the front door of his dwelling, thinking himself alone at the center of the woods—his heart in his eyes; or as one feels spying upon a small animal after it has been chased, and when it thinks itself safe, sits, bunched and still, just breathing.

He was about to leave without disturbing her, when she saw

him. She sat up straight.

"What are *you* doing here? Well, I'm a fool," she said, as he took a seat across from her—"merry-go-riding at my age. And I don't think they had a good time."

"I think they did!" he replied. "It was a wonderful idea!"

"You do?" she asked. "It was?" She asked it in a child's voice.

He said, "I do. Didn't you see Cathy?"

"Yes," she said, "she's lovely when she's gay. She mustn't lose that."

The waitress approached with Nina's dinner. "My gentleman friend is joining me," she said, her voice changing—suddenly harsh, comic. "What are you going to give him to eat?"

"What would he like?" asked the waitress, a round-faced blonde who was really gray.

"Give him the chicken dinner," Nina said. "He needs to get fat."

Miles was scanning the menu. "Filet of sole," he said.

"Pooh," said Nina, "give him the chicken dinner, Rose."

Rose looked calmly from one to the other.

"The sole, please," said Miles.

"Bring him the chicken," said Nina. "Bring him both," she said. "Look at him, he's a runt."

Miles colored.

"Bring him his pale fish," said Nina. "Well," she said, as Rose turned away, "all right, we'll have a lovely dinner. Weren't you nice to come?"

"Awfully," he said. He told her, "I wanted to come, of course."

"It was very nice of you," she stated.

At the end of dinner, she said that she must go straight home. She was tired. "O.K.," he said. But as he started off the straight way home, she told him, "Drive round by the point." A small yacht was moored to the main pier. "Son of a bitch," she exclaimed, "he's dining on board. The menu here isn't fine enough for him." On the pier below, a few old men were out with lanterns and nets, scooping up the next day's bait—the small shrimp that came twitching under in the tide. "Do you know what they're after?" she quizzed him. They rounded the land's end, where the sea wall turned and ended, and the big expensive hotel lay down out over the water. Gulls were crying at its windows. Beyond the hotel, the ocean stretched shiny to the horizon. The moon was up.

Nina cried, "Stop!" He put on the brakes. The moon whitened the water far out, and where the waves curled on the sand they were phosphorescent. A small dog was at the water's edge, sniffing, gingerly stepping, eyeing the flood.

"You really should go in," she told him.

He gave a little shudder. "Might get too bad a burn," he said, and grinned at her. "May the sun not burn me by day, nor the moon by night."

"Come on," she said, "bed time."

He started up the car again. She turned to him abruptly. "And how does it hurt to be burned?" she asked.

He gave her a startled and suddenly timid look, and didn't answer.

That night Cathy and Andy were up twice with Rick, and before breakfast two tourist women appeared at the door, seeking lodging. The household was in a state of peculiar agitation. "They've been up and down stairs more times than I can count," Nina wrote to her husband. "One trip for sheets and another for pillow cases, another with towels and another with washcloths, I suppose. And a special trip with a tiny bouquet snatched from the garden patch and thrust in triumph into some little vase they've searched through all the cupboards for. Oh, they are children! And I, damn it, am a fool. Robert, I am a fool. Yesterday. . . ." She wrote him about her impulsive outing with them. "Oh, now I am lost. That boy wants to be my friend now, I know it."

She was correct, of course. About two o'clock that day, lying out in the sun, she sat up and peered down the beach. There he was, standing idly at the water's edge, just not looking in her direction. When she stood up, he promptly turned her way and she beckoned to him. He was in swimming shorts and he had his shirt and pants and shoes over his shoulder. She watched him curiously as he approached. He moved always as though he were stiff, as though he were containing himself carefully; as though he would like to run, to skip, to jump, but were afraid that his motions might take him, of their own accord, to some strange place.

He greeted her with embarrassment: "It's me."

"Yes, I see it's you," she told him.

He stood before her as though waiting for instructions.

"Sit down," she told him.

He sat.

"How's your work going?" she asked. "Are you getting a lot done?"

He looked surprised. He threw a handful of sand at his shoes. "Yes, a certain amount," he said.

"Are you pleased with it?" she asked him.

He said, "I don't know."

She began to question him further. With whom had he studied? He answered in abstracted fashion, so she stopped her questions. He built a sand fort upon his extended left foot, and then shook it down. She waited. He restlessly scattered more sand upon his body, burying both legs; then shook it all off. She sat, watching him, frowning slightly, her head tilted as if to listen for some small sound. Her hands rested, quiet, upon the sand. In her stillness she resembled a sphinx, planted there beside the waves.

He sighed suddenly. He asked her, "You know me, don't you?"

She raised her eyebrows at him. "Know you?"

"Tell my fortune," he demanded.

She laughed. She chided him, "That's for you to tell." But he sat there waiting. She relented toward him: "I think you have a wonderful fortune. I thought so the first time I saw you."

"Ha!" he said. But then suddenly he turned on her such a look of denial that she asked, startled, "What is it?"

He glanced about him, and then sighed again, as though from some tremendous exertion.

"Say it," she said. "What is it?"

A gull landed near them, letting down his feet and running his springy walk toward them, hoping probably for bread; stopped, hunchback, and regarded them with his lacquered eyes.

"And what are *you* looking at?" said Miles.

The gull cocked his head at him, then walked down to the water's edge and pecked at a branch of seaweed.

Nina waited again in silence. Finally she asked, "Do you live alone, back home, or with your family?"

"I have a room," he said, "but I probably shouldn't."

Why shouldn't he? she asked. Well, he said, it was hard on his mother. She was divorced. His brother lived in Detroit.

"You probably live with her all too much as it is," she told him.

He smiled. "Now I remember your feelings about parents," he said. "But you can't really blame me on my mother."

"Oh, maybe I could," she said, and uttered one harsh note of laughter.

"We'll have some refreshments," she said. She took from her basket two oranges, and peeled them and broke them into segments and laid them on a towel. "Eat." He ate his orange, spitting out the seeds in the direction of the gull, who sidestepped.

"You should eat all of these you can," she told him. "Do you?"

He stared at her. "Oranges?"

"Yes," she said. "I think you need vitamins. You're tan but you're sallow under the tan."

He laughed.

"What's funny?" she asked him.

"I'm sorry," he said. "But you *are* somebody's mother, aren't you?"

She was annoyed.

He scooped a careful hole in the sand and buried the peel of the two oranges. Nina watched him closely. She resumed her questions.

"Does your mother support you?"

He told her that a year ago his father's mother had left him six thousand dollars.

"Wonderful," she said.

Yes, he said, he was lucky. It gave him a few years' grace in which to prove himself.

She exploded. "What do you mean?"

"As a sculptor," he said.

She sat up straight. "How ridiculous! One has one's life in which to prove oneself. What's the meaning of such a deadline?"

"Well," he said, "of course." He frowned. "The point is—neither of my parents thinks it makes much sense." He stopped her: "I know it's my own life. And they don't try to prevent me. But they think I should have another profession on the side. And they worry because they feel I should be equipping myself right now—and keep that money as security. Every time Mother sends me a check, she makes some little comment—."

"Sends you a check?" she cried.

He was getting flustered. Of course, he told her, it was his money. But it was in his mother's bank, just for convenience, and she—

"Really!" she cried. "What's convenient about that? I never heard of anything so outrageous. It's your money. She shouldn't have anything to do with it. You're a big enough boy to write your own checks, aren't you?"

He knew, he said. It would have been better in his own name. He'd thought of suggesting that they change it, but he didn't want to hurt her feelings, and it would.

She shook her head, her mouth clamped tight shut. They were facing each other there, he on his knees, in his excitement, and she sitting up so straight that she sat almost as tall.

"But I did write her just last week," he cried, "that she had to allow it to be mine, and not always question my spending it. I told her that she had to believe a little in what I was doing or, I said, I couldn't live. I spoke very frankly."

She raged: "No! No!"

He folded back on his knees, to a sitting position again. He began to fidget with the laces of his shoes, flung down beside him.

"Good lord," she told him, "you had no right to write such a letter! It's not for your mother to give you your life! She did that once! And once is enough for her! It's yours to *take up* now! It's yours to *tell* her that it's yours—not to beg but to take it, take it!" She gestured in the air with snatching hands: "Take it!" Now she seemed a gorgon with wild locks, with fiery eye and tongue; and he seemed transfixed before her, consumed in that fire.

He tried to stammer, "Yes but—"

"If you hurt her," she raged, "it's too bad. You must be willing to hurt her. If you hurt her, you hurt her. It hurt to bring you into the world. These things are natural."

"Oh, I shall hurt her enough," he said—and glanced his eyes about him.

She gave him a quick narrow look and sat again very still.

He turned to stare at the small waves hissing upon the sand. His gaze grew passive. "My mother," he said—with a soft shrug of his shoulders, a little unfamiliar motion, unwitting, that summoned up for Nina his mother, her shoulders sliding forward in the same soft gesture of stubborn resignation. He began to tell his mother's story— began to tell all there had been to hurt his mother, down through the years. The climax of the story was his father's infatuation with a mere girl whom he had met on a ship, returning from a business trip. An infatuation was all it was, but his mother had been so hurt, and so proud, that she had forced a divorce, and his father had married the girl. *She* had abandoned *him* within the year. If only—

Nina stopped him: "Yes," she said, "yes, don't tell me any more. I know, I know. And you're moping about, feeling that if only you could play your role correctly, were loving enough and patient, you could mend their lives, speak the marriage words over them all over again. Good God, good God!" she cried. "Over and over I've seen this! Children should not have to have parents!" She demanded, "Did you ever read *The Way of All Flesh*? Read it," she said, "read it. Children should be born, he says, the way a certain insect—I forget what insect—but the parents lay the egg, leave food enough for the baby to nibble when it hatches, until it's big enough to want to fly about for its own, and then they *die*." She stressed the word with a violent jerk of her head. "The child doesn't ever have to lay eyes on them! A baby should be born, Butler says, a human baby, wrapped in a large bank note. And then the parents should go away!" she raged. "Really, they should all die on the spot!"

She was possessed. She was exultant. Her face shone. "Over and over," she repeated, "I've seen children trying to live out their parents' lives. They throw away their own. Oh, it's as old as literature, of course. The Greeks were writing about it." Abruptly she began to speak of neighbors of hers. "Their eldest daughter—she's a real Elektra. A bright and beautiful girl, who's never done anything, and never will marry. She hangs around that house, still, with vengeance in her eye. Whether it's blessings you'd work or vengeance, it's all one! Her mother divorced her father and married his partner. A silly vulgar man. Stupid of her. But it was her mother's wrong. The girl will be living it out all her life."

Another example came to her. He listened, amazed and meek, as she spread before him the dramas of these various lives. She turned again to his. "You tell your mother's story with more passion than you do your own. You have your own life. You can't take as your profession the mending of your mother's life!"

"I don't," he muttered.

"Oh," she cried, "you can't deny it. It's there, as you speak, in your passion—"

"All right," he said.

She stopped. She stared him in the eye. "Take up your own life, Miles!"

He smiled at her a pallid smile. He looked down at his hands, as though he must literally take up his life in them. And he let them turn palm downward.

She asked more quietly, "Your own life eludes you?"

He shut his eyes.

"My dear boy," she said. Across her face passed an expression of tenderness that was almost exaltation.

He opened his eyes and sat up, straightening his legs out before him. He looked down at himself—his eyes travelling the length of himself as though he wished that under that look his body would evaporate. With a gesture of his hands he disdained himself.

She whispered, "You wish that you were sexless—is that it?"

He jerked his head, yes.

"And why?" she asked him.

He didn't answer.

She asked, "Because you are homosexual?"

He smiled.

"There," she said, "it is said. And the sky hasn't fallen." She asked, "Do you think you are the only one?"

"No," he said, "and there are the starving Armenians."

"What do you mean by that?" she asked.

"I mean," he began.

She interrupted him: "And why can't you live with it? It's no death sentence."

He bowed his head, and then he looked up at her again. She sat watching him gravely—so still, so infinitely attentive, that she seemed again some ancient image stumbled upon, there in the sands. He began to tell his history.

He told her of first love. Then, he said, love had seemed simple. The man had been one of his highschool teachers—a kind of pagan, of great charm, whose god was Desire. To lie in his arms had seemed very natural. "Like living in the Garden of Eden," Miles said. "But one can never remain in that garden, of course." He smiled wanly. His voice had fallen into an odd almost stilted cadence, as though he were reciting. In college, he told her, he had fallen in love with a fellow student. "He made a gesture of love toward me, and so I made a gesture of love toward him. And then I saw that he was frightened for his life. So I spared his life." He muttered on, telling of uneasy love.

"But then," he said, "there are others one begins to meet. There is a certain look." He squinted at her. "There you are. We know you.

One of us. But they mean us, us," he said. He was grimacing now. "I'll belong to no club." He stopped. "I say that easily. But I belong. But won't and can't," he labored. "But there is a funny pull to that look. One can't help wanting to be known." He gave himself a shake. "One moves through so many days in false face. Even with my family, my close friends. At my brother's wedding, they all hit me on the back—'Your turn next.' To unmask to them would be stupid, and unkind. Anyway, it's not a public matter. And yet—to *be* recognized—"

He moved his shoulders vaguely. "It's a funny relief. To join their company. Can you see? And so I have," he said wryly. "But I can't." He muttered on. Nina listened, rapt. "I won't join any club.

And I also won't terrify anybody with my love. So what is there to do?" he said violently. "Diet on saltpeter." He laughed. She winced, at that. He jumped up, scattering sand from him.

She nodded at him. "Listen—go and take a dip. Then come back and let me say something to you."

She put her hands over her eyes for a moment, as though to catch a nap, but then looked after him. He waded out slowly, staring all about him, as though he could perhaps summon from the wave the life that eluded him. He thrust himself in—then thrashed about him as though it were freezing cold. He came back and flung himself down beside her. "Wash us," he murmured, "and comb us. And set us on the bank to dry."

"Here," she said, and handed him her towel.

He declined it.

"Dry your hair at least," she told him. She took the towel and dried it, roughly, for him. He got to his knees.

"You know, you need a haircut," she told him.

"Oh?" he asked.

"Listen," she said, putting the towel down and sitting back. "There is only one thing that deforms you. Fear. Let me speak." He had raised his eyebrows at her. She told him, "I have watched you. You move in fear."

They sat, facing each other, each peering into the other's face, like idol and worshipper, oracle and one who has come a long distance to ask his fate. As they were talking, the two tourist women who had arrived that morning walked by, along the tideline, picking up shells.

"Wait," Miles said to Nina.

"They can't hear," she chided him.

The two women passed, turning their faces under their sun hats, staring in spite of themselves because the two sat so rapt. The first woman had been about to stoop and pick up a brilliant conch, of a plaid design that seemed to her unusual. But something in the attitudes of the two up the beach made her stop her hand and hurry by, instead. The second woman, not so easily awed, took the shell.

"You see," Nina told Miles, "you're afraid they'll hear some word we say. What if they do?"

"Well," he said, "they're not looking for souvenirs like that."

But she sat stern and concentrated. She told him, "You're afraid to upset people. And you're afraid to upset yourself. You're afraid to fall—and be dirtied." She frowned at him, sitting there very shiny-skinned. She told him, "You are an artist. Nothing was ever created out of caution." She scooped up a fist full of sand. "Miles, what makes a pearl?"

Miles tried again to make her smile. "An oyster has an upset stomach?" he asked.

She took no notice. "All right," she said, "a little sand gets in his shell. The pearl is this dirt, is this irritation." She said, "Don't smile. It's out of that which soils us, which irritates, which rubs—it's out of evil suffered and understood—that an artist creates."

Down the beach, the two women hunting shells turned for a moment to peer back at them. And above their heads the gull, joined by another gull, hung, treading air, crying out for a crumb to eat.

At the same hour again the next day, Miles joined Nina on the beach. Overnight there had been a high sea; the water's surface was still ruffled into white. "Peeling the green," the fishermen called it. "Did you know that?" Nina asked Miles. He didn't. He asked her to walk all the way down with him around the point; she should see the beach there. He'd just seen it from a distance, but a passing ship must have had most of its cargo washed off deck.

They started off together. The shore was festooned with kelp. Small crabs were entangled in its garlands, and the sand was stained as if by wine. "It's always festive after a high sea," she said. She smiled at him gayly. He smiled back at her. But as they walked on, he grew silent and fidgety. "You know, Nina—."

She asked, "What is it?"

He said, "One thing I perhaps shouldn't have said to you yesterday."

Her face clouded, and she stopped.

He said, "I spoke to you about Stanley. I really shouldn't have named him. Because—"

She cut him short, haughty and crisp. "Miles, I didn't ask you to confide in me, you know—to tell me the things that you did. You wanted someone to talk to and I listened. If you regret it now—" Her face was dark and pinched.

He touched her arm. "Nina, wait."

But she raved at him. "I didn't go prying. I didn't come down here to get mixed up in other people's lives. I came down here to be alone and to work. You came to me. You wanted to unburden yourself. So—"

"Please please please!" he cried.

She stopped.

He exclaimed, "If you think I regret!"

She asked, "No?" She spoke suddenly in a small unsteady voice.

"Shall I tell you," he said, "how I *do* feel?"

She stood like an apprehensive child one is coaxing, but who expects in a moment to be struck.

He said, "When I left you after dinner—" He interrupted himself. "When I came down here," he said, "before I met you— You were right about me." He made a face. He threw out his hands as if to grasp for words. "I used to lie awake at night and listen to the waves breaking. They sounded much too loud." He broke off, incoherently. He tried again. "Last night," he said, "I went into the bathroom. As I came in, I saw a spider on the wall. I hate spiders. When I was a child—" Again he interrupted himself. He said, "I took off my shoe to swat it." He peered at her. "But then I didn't swat it. I washed without bothering that he was sitting up there." His eyes shone at her. "I very nearly wished him goodnight."

She was straining for the relevance of his words, frowning, her face puckered.

He made a gesture of impatience with himself. "I'm sorry," he said. "That sounds silly. I'm not telling you. I'm trying to say—" He shifted his voice to a lower pitch, because it had started to tremble. "I am trying to say that you have given me back to life."

At his final words, her brow leapt up, her eyes filling with tears, her face abruptly smoothed, strangely gleaming. She whispered to him, "Thank you." He opened his mouth and she interrupted him: "All right." She gave her head a shake.

She asked, "Where is this shipwreck I should see?" She took him by the hand.

These two became inseparable now. They met each day toward the middle of the afternoon and spent the rest of the day together. They swam, or roamed about the town of Fiddler, or sat on the sea wall, letting the town pass in front of them; or sometimes they set off in his car to explore new territories. "It's a honeymoon," said Mrs. Bruce slyly, hoping to provoke her daughter into telling her just what was between the woman—who was certainly fifty?—and the boy. Cathy only stared at her with surprise and reproof. One could never learn anything from a daughter.

It *was* for both of them a little like a honeymoon. For Nina, deprived of the celebration she had expected when her novel came out (she thought it her best book, and she had anticipated felicitations, feasting, society), Miles's appreciation of her now made up a little for that missed time. Nina's very first novel had brought her a taste of fame; but though in the years that followed, her talent had not waned, her work had never again won the same kind of acclaim. With this last book she had expected, in spite of everything, to be taken note of again. Miles read her book and gave the response she had hoped for from the critics. It was a novel about a young girl, overborne by her loving family. The elements were familiar to him. Miles's approval of Nina was unstinted. He was charmed by her. She could astonish him endlessly.

He showed her his work and she was more impressed than she

had expected to be. His sculpture surprised her by its force, though it was uncontrolled still and a bit agonized. "You must learn not to try so hard," she told him. "Lawrence says 'Cease to care, cease to care.'" And the sense that she could help him toward life revived her own self-assurance.

For Miles, meeting Nina had indeed almost literally recalled him to life. In her company the world about him, through which he had been moving enclosed in anxieties as in a cloud, became suddenly visible, populated. He was of an amiable disposition and tended to find people likeable until they were proved the contrary. Before her coming, he had walked through the town smiling pleasantly at whomever his eyes happened to rest upon. He knew a good many of the inhabitants by sight. But what their lives were or why they had come here, in what dramas they were caught up, he had never thought to wonder. For him, here they were, simply—like the sea, the sand, the shells along the beach. In Nina's company they suddenly acquired human histories.

For instance, in the Paradise one evening, Nina told Miles to fill up the jukebox with nickels; the waitress, Rose, was going to show them the cakewalk. "Come on, Rose, the sheriff is at the other end of town." Miles was astonished to hear that Rose had that talent, and just as astonished at Nina's knowing that she had. "Why? We both talk English," Nina told him. Years before, Rose had been a vaudeville hoofer. She had come down here with an ailing husband, and he had died, and she had stayed on. Rose stepped into the cakewalk with very little persuasion; and halfway through the dance, Nina got up and joined her, in an inaccurate but lively imitation of the steps. As the record ended, she and Rose embraced like long-lost sisters, Nina exultant.

Many of those upon whom Miles used to smile, without thinking, became now suddenly and dramatically the enemy. The scene acquired violent light and shade, for Nina was full of passionate judgements. The sheriff was a bully. The pretty lady in the real estate

office had ruined one of the best fishermen on the coast. Nina sus-
pected that there was something between her now and the owner of
the yacht. He was a disgusting person, too. Such airs. "Wouldn't you
like to ask us on board?" Nina had called to him one day. He had
pretended not to hear. All the rich tourists at the big hotel were foe.
When Nina and Miles walked past the lot where their shiny cars
were drawn up, Nina would kick at their fenders, or if she and Miles
were driving by, she would say to him, "Just take a little nick out of
one of them." And he would feint at one, for her pleasure, and she
would hoot with laughter, and the car's owner, if present, would stare
haughtily, or call out, "Watch it, there!"

They did foolish things together, quite as young lovers might. To
each this time brought a new energy that brimmed over into foolish-
ness. Miles, at ease, was exuberant and reckless. This delighted Nina.
One evening he drove her down along the beach, pretending that it
was the beach at Daytona, and got the car stuck deep in the sand.
Another evening when there was phosphorescence in the waves, he
seized Nina's hand and ran with her into the surf, before she could
resist him. Nina was wearing a jersey skirt, which shrank above her
knees. They had to slip her back into the house without anyone seeing her.

"Nevermore!" said Nina—more than once—"I'm too old!" But to
her husband she wrote of these adventures with pride. She teased
him, "You should really be jealous."

She and Miles were not always alone. Sometimes they persuaded one or more of the Fullers to come along, or even Mrs. Bruce.
Or they took Rose, on her day off. Occasionally now they ate with the
Fullers, who were always urging it. Nina was anxious not to seem to
be stealing Miles from them.

Lately the Fullers had been almost animated. The two tourist
women hadn't stayed for many days, and they were celebrating their
departure. "It's so wonderfully peaceful without them," Andy said.
"My son-in-law has the real business instinct," said Mrs. Bruce. They

were celebrating, too, the expected advent of two friends—Roger White, a painter, and his wife, a writer, Sydney Hollis. "I just hope there won't be any tourists the week *they're* here," said Andy. What the Fullers obviously really wanted their house to be was not a tourist inn but an Art Center. The Whites were on their way to Key West—the setting Sydney intended for her next series of stories. She had just been awarded a handsome fellowship.

"All right," Nina told Miles. "And while they're here, you stick around. Because these are the sort of people you should know. They're professional—which is what you have to learn to be. Yes," she said, "soon I'll be losing you to the new arrivals."

"You will not be losing me," said Miles. He said, "Nina, what am I going to do when we each have to go back home?"

"Nonsense," she exclaimed. But she was pleased.

"Yesterday," Miles said, "I was trying to imagine your husband."

"Him!" she exclaimed. "He's impossible! An impossible man!" she said proudly. "Quite sufficient to himself. That's why I married him," she said, "because he didn't really care whether I did or didn't." And she sighed. Her sigh mingled satisfaction and frustration.

The afternoon of the day on which the Whites were to arrive, the jungle bordering the Fullers' house caught fire. A neighbor, burning trash, hadn't bothered to keep the flames under control. It was an old story down here. "It'll clean out the mosquitoes and the snakes," bystanders would drawl. Things grew up again so easily. But the Fullers, being Yankees, had the feeling that one went out and battled a fire; and they were a little concerned for their house, which was protected from the flames only by their driveway. So they got out there, Andy with a shovel and Cathy with an old tennis racket, and started beating at it. Soon after, Nina and Miles turned up.

"The best thing to use is brooms!" Nina shouted at them.

"Please, not my new broom!" Mrs. Bruce called from the house.

Miles found a rake, and Nina emptied the broom closet, but left

behind the new broom. "Always self contained, that woman, do you
see?" she muttered to Miles. "Thinks of her new broom. Here, take
the tennis racket away from that poor girl and give her this!"

The blaze leapt from bush to bush, hissing where it alit.

"Here!" cried Nina. "We can cut it off from here! No, over
here!"

She took over the battle.

The wind was not strong and after about an hour, they had the
fire almost under control. But the Fullers began to look at their
watches. The Whites were due at six.

"I was going to have some flowers in their room," Cathy said,
"and maybe find a different bedspread." Andy had been going to town
for a bottle of gin.

"I wouldn't fret," Nina called to them. "They can rough it for
one day."

But they still cast at each other distracted glances. Cathy began
to find dead frogs in her path—singed in the act of leaping for safe
ground. "Oh!" she would exclaim, and put down her broom to stare
unhappily at each stiff little creature. Then she would sigh again, "I
had wanted to arrange some flowers."

By a little after five o'clock, one small patch of fire remained.
Cathy looked at her watch again and said, "I don't think it'll do much
harm now, do you?"

Andy leaned on his shovel and held up a finger to the wind.
"Shouldn't think this wind would take it far." The remnant of the
fire made a small lapping sound. "Sounds tamed to me," said Andy.

"You're a fool," Nina shouted at him. "Your guests aren't *that*
special."

Cathy and Andy drew near each other and mumbled together.

Miles said, "Go on, if you like. Nina and I will kill the last of
it."

"I should say not," said Nina.

"Come on," said Andy, "We've tamed it. Everybody quit."

Miles chanted, " 'The fire saith not, It is enough!' "

Cathy and Andy were already hurrying to the house.

"Listen," Nina said to Miles. "Come on—give them a lift to town. They're in a state."

She spoke sharply. Miles put down his rake. "Want to come along?" he asked her.

"I'm going to nap," Nina said. She looked suddenly very drawn and weary.

Nina slept more heavily than she had expected to. She woke from her nap abruptly, hearing voices in the house. The Whites had arrived and were being shown about. For a moment, *all* the voices sounded to her like the voices of new arrivals. She identified what must be Sydney Hollis's voice—low, slow, in control. But for a moment, then, she took Andy's voice to be Roger White's. It was not in its usual register, or at its usual pace. Andy was sounding lively. She heard someone speak who must be Roger. His voice was pleasant, silken, boyish. She heard Miles laugh—a sudden easy explosion of laughter. And she pursed her brow. Roger's voice slid on again. And again Miles relaxed into laughter.

Nina rose from her bed. She was invited to dinner to meet the Whites, but she was anxious to slip out of the house for a little walk, before having to confront them. She went to her window and peered out. She grimaced. While she had slept, a little wind had risen and the patch of flames they had abandoned had been puffed the whole extent of the woods that bordered the house. The entire strip lay black. Even a bit of their lawn had been singed.

She dressed quickly and, listening first at her door, tiptoed downstairs and out, unseen. She walked alongside the ruin, sniffing the smoky air. A thin fall of ashes was settling—like talcum, or light snow. From some of the taller pines and palms, showers of sparks were still dropping, desultorily. She muttered, "Stupid, stupid," and turned back to the house.

As she was coming up the path, the front door opened and the whole company stepped out onto the porch. Nina's eyes flicked to the Whites. They were an oddly matched pair—he very tall, and exuberant in manner, rather homely (his nose was crooked, his ears prominent) but of such vivid coloring that he seemed handsome; she much smaller than he, with a lean and contained look, neat features, short taffy-colored hair.

Miles caught sight of Nina. "There she is!"

Andy asked, with an embarrassed smile, "Have you been surveying the damage?"

"Ha!" she snorted. "I hope your guests appreciate that it was in their honor."

Miles turned to the Whites—"They laid down the red carpet for you."

The Whites smiled upon him.

Drinks were set out on a silver tray which Nina had never seen in use. There were anchovies. And Cathy had managed to arrange two bouquets. On the dining room table, Nina noticed a lace tablecloth.

Mrs. Bruce was feeding Ricky his supper in the kitchen. Hearing their voices, Nina suddenly headed in there. "We three will have our own party! Well, aren't things dolled up?" she said to Mrs. Bruce.

"Aren't they?" Mrs. Bruce agreed.

Nina joked with them until Miles came looking for her.

Roger loved to talk, was full of tales even at the end of a tedious journey. Collapsing into his chair, stretching out his legs, he opened his mouth to yawn, and upon the yawn followed a humorous tale, and then another. He uttered them as another traveller might slap the dust from his coat sleeves. The Fullers sat enchanted. And so did Miles, Nina noted. Roger did most of the talking, but it was Sydney round whom the chairs were drawn, automatically. And as Roger talked, he turned to her, as a singer turns to the prompter. She gave, as if were, permission. The Fullers, too, looked faithfully her way—in the middle of a laugh, the middle of a nod—to check whether she was laughing, nodding, too. Nina saw Miles adopting the same motion. Sydney had the magnetism of the very self-possessed.

"How's New York?" the Fullers asked.

"Roger, tell them how New York is," said Sydney. "Get me a cigarette first." She smiled at them all. Roger began to describe their departure in a snow storm.

They had almost missed their train. "We left for the station at an unreasonably reasonable hour. Freddie Tate was seeing us off and you know what a mother hen he is." The Fullers nodded. Roger imitated Freddie clucking them into a cab. Then he summoned the storm before them, with hands in the air and violently fluttering fingers. By 37th Street, traffic was so stalled they'd decided to try it on foot. Freddie had reached for their bags, of course, but they didn't think he'd possibly make it. "He's rounder than ever," said Roger. "I tell him, 'They can't call *you* a minor critic!' "

Miles, laughing, looked round at Nina.

They'd battled their way to the station alone. "But just before we pulled out, there came Freddie, puffing down the platform—"

"Ah, Freddie," said Sydney. "What a friend!"

The Fullers nodded.

"Ha!" Nina suddenly brought her feet down onto the floor with a kind of pounce. "Actually, he's a real bastard. I'm sorry to have to tell you."

Sydney stared.

"He's nobody's friend. I'm sorry. He's for himself."

"Better mind her warnings," Miles announced possessively. "She's a kind of gypsy, a witch."

Sydney looked startled. She had a face that lit up, full of charm, almost elfin, when she felt approved of, but froze, homely and severe, too muscular, when she felt assailed. But Roger laughed. "Poor Freddie. He's been good to *us*."

"Yes, he knows why," said Nina. "Don't count on it. A *very* minor critic," she added. Then suddenly she retired into herself, as if wishing that she could pretend to herself that she had never spoken.

Mrs. Bruce joined them at dinner. She turned to Sydney. "Andy gave me your book to read, Miss Hollis. I was terribly impressed. But I confess I couldn't finish it. Modern books are too clever for me, they're over my head."

Nina muttered another exclamation: "Ha! I'll give you mine to read. It's just a story. I'm of your generation."

Miles raised his eyebrows at her. "Well, hardly just a story."

"My fan," she said, nodding at him.

"Yes," said Mrs. Bruce, "two authoresses at table! Are writers supposed to get along with each other?"

"Oh, never, never," said Nina.

"Why some of my best friends—" said Sydney lightly.

"Never, never," said Nina. "Speak the truth. As writers, truth is our concern."

Roger laughed, but Sydney, again, froze, her face veiling over, aloof and watchful.

"We should have your book in the house, too," Andy said to Nina.

Nina seemed not to have heard him.

Roger continued talkative. And more and more he turned for audience to Miles. Miles had a little the quality of a shy precocious child. He didn't speak very often, but he followed every motion made and every word spoken with an extraordinary attentiveness. He didn't always understand what was happening around him. He had been too occupied with questions about himself to have acquired any sure knowledge of other people. He responded in a social situation as many people respond to music—feelingly, blindly. But he always responded. He was a good audience. Both Roger and Sydney kept glancing at him, with curiosity and pleasure. Nina watched, her eyes travelling from one to the other.

"I forgot to give you a message from Jim Blair," Roger said to

Miles. "He says you're not to stay down here too long. He asked us to dig for you in the beach and send you back north." He squinted at Miles. "I see what he meant." Miles was by now a sooty tan and his hair had been very much bleached by the sun.

Sydney said, "You do begin to blur with the landscape."

They all stared at him. *"Boy in Landscape,"* said Andy, smiling at Sydney. This had been the title of one of her most successful stories.

"Son of a beach," said Roger.

Everybody laughed except Nina. She was suddenly very solemn.

They were interrupted by a thin cry from above. Rick had awakened. Both Cathy and Andy went hurrying upstairs, and came back down with him. He had been having a nightmare. Andy took him in his lap. "What were you dreaming, Rick?" he asked him.

"The moon," the boy said. "The brown moon come look in my window."

"The moon isn't brown," his father told him. "You were dreaming. What color is the moon?"

"Brown moon," said the boy. "Look in my window."

"The moon is white," Andy told him patiently.

"That's a surprising statement from a painter," said Sydney.

Rick hid his head inside his father's jacket and lay still.

"Truth is my concern," said Andy.

Roger began, at that, to quiz Andy about the colors of various objects in the room. "That chair against the wall, for example."

"Purple and orange," said Andy, to elude him.

"That's not so far off," said Roger.

"I know, it's an eyesore," said Andy.

Mrs. Bruce spoke up. "That's my great-grandmother's chair. What's ugly about it?"

Roger winked at Miles.

"For instance, what color is Miles's hair?" Nina suddenly interjected.

They all, again, stared at him.

"Green," Roger said.

And Nina suddenly asked Roger: "Why don't you paint him?"

Roger raised his eyebrows. But then he turned to Sydney. She nodded. "You should."

Nina sat straight in her chair, at attention.

When Roger turned toward him, Miles smiled, but he did not speak. Nina spoke for him, "He'd be delighted. Look at him."

"Would you want to sit tomorrow?" Roger asked.

"He's very disciplined and works every morning," Nina broke in. "He'll pose for you after lunch."

Sydney said, "Do paint it as a landscape. Put him on the sand, with shells and driftwood."

"And a few dead fish," contributed Andy, who then warmed to the subject. "Bury him up to his eyes."

Ricky had brought his head out from cover. "Not to do it," he said.

"Thank you, Rick," said Miles.

Ricky began to cry. Cathy rushed at him to gather him up. "Want Miles to put me to bed," he announced. So Miles shouldered him.

As he mounted the stairs with Ricky, "He's very charming," Sydney said.

"He's the best," Nina interjected firmly. And her voice now contained, suddenly, a warning note.

Nina had named, as the hour at which Miles would sit for Roger, the very hour at which Miles and she were accustomed to meet. With this evening, the routine of their days together was broken. There began a new and strange time between them.

The difference was marked almost immediately. When Miles turned up to pose, Roger suggested a walk first. On the walk, they met Nina. "Painter getting in the mood," said Roger. Miles opened his mouth to say something, but then shut it again. Nina was peering at them like the ancient seer on the street corner, who will then shriek out, "Beware!" or "The time has arrived!" Not that she called out anything. She held her tongue. But Miles and Roger walked on no longer chatting—even Roger, usually full of words, subdued to self-consciousness.

After the sitting, Miles went to look for Nina, but she had left for town, though it was early still. He picked her up in the road, walking. She looked surprised and, he thought, not very glad to see him.

"Didn't they ask you to stay for dinner?" she asked.

He told her, "I said I was eating with you." He spoke tensely, disconcerted by her manner.

She said quickly, "I didn't expect you." She was remote. She didn't look at him directly. For the first time, he felt awkward with her.

The next day, Roger invited everybody to go out for dinner. But Nina made some excuse to decline. Miles drove the others to Carefree. "She's a violent person, your friend," Sydney remarked. Roger said, "I like her. She's unexpected."

The painting took several days. When he was through posing, Miles would go looking for Nina; but very often he couldn't find her. She wouldn't be in any of the accustomed places. But the Whites would be there at the house when he returned, and so he would go off somewhere with them. Nina had suggested to them the first evening that Miles could take them about in his car. They had been asking about a certain pond in which one could sometimes see alligators. "Miles will drive you there," she had volunteered. And when Sydney had spoken of her wish to see St. Petersburg, she had spoken up again—"Miles will take you." Miles found himself abandoning Nina. He felt confused. It seemed to him that she conspired to be abandoned. Unsure of her, and too self conscious—fretting over whether she kept out of his way because she assumed that he preferred the Whites or because she tired of his company—when he did see her, he urged their next-day meetings with a hesitant and strained air. She turned snappish—"We'll see. Tomorrow's another day."

When they were together now, he felt awkward if he talked about the Whites, and he felt awkward if he didn't. Nina herself would often abruptly introduce the subject. She would ask, "Well, where did you go with them? Did you have a good time?" Or she would ask, "What is she working on now?" But then when he began to tell about where they had been, or to reply to her question about Sydney, she would suddenly appear savagely bored. Or she would listen with interest, but with such an air of one who anticipates the outrageous, that he would ask himself: What am I saying? Formerly her presence had granted Miles a curious release. He had felt at ease with himself, able to move upon impulse and to speak without hesitating—suddenly graceful; felt like the one in the fairy tale over whom the fairy has flicked her wand and when he opens his mouth gold coins tumble from it, to his astonishment. But now he felt like the one who opens his mouth and—to his astonishment—toads jump out.

Miles looked to Nina to let him know how to restore the relation that had been between them. But, naturally, she refused to prompt him.

So Miles spent more and more time with the Whites. On the beach, he and Roger enjoyed themselves together like little boys. They dug enormous tunnels in the sand, or they built enormous castles, or they erected statues of sand that were very elaborate, with shells for eyes, nose, mouth, with feathers for hair. Or they buried each other. Or, when Andy came along, they buried Andy. Sydney would sit, surveying the scene, reading, or else sunning herself, browning methodically. They played before her rather as jugglers or acrobats at a royal court, aware of her always as their audience. They also fetched her shells for her collection. She was collecting the very delicate shells, or those stones which were precisely symmetrical. To be with them was pleasant for Miles, yet it was also vaguely disturbing. He felt in their company a little captive, a little less than himself. To be as a child again was agreeable, yet not agreeable, and he retained toward them an instinctive reserve.

When Nina's eye was upon him, however, he did not know what it was that he felt toward the Whites. He felt estranged from them by her look, which was so distinctly critical of them. He felt at the same time, and by that same look, curiously more bound to them than he would like.

Though Nina declined every invitation to join the company for dinner again, sometimes she did join them for drinks. One day the talk turned to Key West. "You really should come with us, Miles," Roger said, "if you've never been there. Don't you think so, Sydney? Besides," he said with a smile, "that would give us a chauffeur."

Nina seemed to prick up her ears. Her brow leapt up as a dog's ears leap up—and all the skin of her face.

"Very good, sir," Miles replied. He was flustered. Aware of Nina, he supposed, suddenly, that she supposed that he might go off with them. The idea became more real to him when he thought of her thinking this than it could have of its own power. A slight thrill passed through him. He supposed, suddenly, that she supposed that he was in love with Roger. And in that instant he almost was.

From the moment that he felt this, he began to experience resentment both of the Whites and of Nina. From the beginning he had been attracted by Roger, but in a vague and uncomplicated fashion. Now he found him fascinating suddenly, and unpleasantly so. He grew very wary with him. He disliked the helplessness he now felt in his presence. He was very curiously adrift. It was not so much Roger's own power over him that he struggled to cast off, as the hypnotic image of what he supposed Nina supposed that power to be. He wished sometimes violently now that he had never confided in Nina. What she was imagining began to obsess him.

Nina's exact thoughts were hard to know. Her behavior was bewildering. When she appeared among them, she usually sat in the

chair nearest the door, and sat on its edge, ready to take flight. Sometimes, even, she remained standing, leaning against the chair's back,
or roamed about the room, examining the bric-a-brac. When she
spoke, it was usually to attack. Often it was something that Sydney
had said that provoked her. In Nina's presence, Sydney soon sat at an
unbecoming round-the-clock guard.

Sydney would remark that she had been reading a certain novel.
"I've been elbowing my way through. What a congested book."

Nina would interject: "Ha! Yes, you have to elbow your way
though. All those characters! His books are like modern cities. Too
many people live there. There is too much noise. You want to slam
the book shut, just as you want to push up out of the subway, run up
into the air again. But—the noise is real, the people are real. Our
latest crop of writers—oh, it's all very ordered and shipshape, nobody
steps on anybody's toes, there's no shoving and pushing and disturb-
ance of the peace. It's exquisite. It's spun glass and all blown out so
cleverly. And you flick it with your fingernail and—excuse me!" she
would conclude—as Sydney paled, the Fullers, nervous and dazzled,
broke into uncomfortable laughter, and Miles pulled in his eyes, to
look at nobody.

Roger alone was quite at his ease. "Listen to her!" He was fasci-
nated by Nina as by some unusual display of fireworks.

Sydney was not Nina's only target. Almost anything that anybody said might call her into the field. She spoke always as one em-
battled. She stood alone against them all. And there was no crossing
to her side.

Andy would mention a young painter of their acquaintance—
"Poor Phil. . . ."

Nina was roused. "Oh, he makes me tired. Poor Phil! Somebody
has always taken care of Phil and somebody always will. He's in no
peril for his life. And nice things he has to say about those who help
him, too!"

Thinking to escape her fire, Andy concurred. "Yes, he's pretty outrageous about Mrs. Rice." And they all nodded, agreeing with her.

But Nina would not be agreed with. "Well, Mrs. Rice can take it, and she asks for it. Dreadful woman! *Dirty* rich, that's called. She doesn't give him a bit more than just enough to scrape along on, you can be sure. She keeps him a beggar."

They were under her guns still, cross the lines as many times as they might like.

She was often sharp with Miles. If he contributed a remark, "Who told you that?" she would challenge him, or comment, "He doesn't know anything about it," throwing him into angry confusion.

One day Nina inquired about the portrait. Roger had just finished it and he brought it in to show.

Sydney pronounced, "Yes, that really catches him, Roger." The Fullers murmured agreement. Miles was dressed, in the portrait, in blue jeans and a faded shirt, and seated on the beach, looking straight out of the picture at one, with an intent, puzzled gaze.

Miles turned to Nina. She looked toward Roger. "You make him too handsome," she said curtly—as though she could say more, but would not. She added, "And too sweet. He's not so sweet."

Miles flushed, and then looked haughty.

She turned on him. "You're an artist, supposedly. An artist can't be sweet. He must be full of anger, full of the truth."

Sydney looked sidewise at her, with dull eyes.

"Well, I'm sure his mother would like it," Nina said.

Roger stared at the portrait, stared at Miles, put his head back and laughed.

Infected by Roger's laughter, Miles laughed too. Then, self-conscious, he stopped.

Roger took the picture away again. The Fullers automatically glanced toward Sydney. Her eyes averted from Nina's, she stated again, "He's really caught him."

Nina started to hum a little tune to herself, studying some shells on the mantelpiece, and looked at her watch, and soon left.

Nina went about these days with a countenance furious and abstracted, like someone with a problem, or a sorrow, someone plotting. Her aspect was that of a dark bird of prey upon a bough, silent, hunched in itself, but darting with its eye brilliant and baleful glances.

Miles felt abandoned. In her company, he had experienced for a while the strong intoxication of one who is recreated by another—had received from her an image of himself with which he could live. To be her creature had seemed his freedom. It was no longer so. Not that she was inattentive now. He felt her to be always watching him. At the same time elusive and ever-present, if he searched for her, she never seemed to be about, but, thinking himself alone, he would turn his head and there she would be, watching him. But to be watched as she watched him now took back from him all his strength. She seemed to be waiting for something to happen, and for something of which she disapproved. She regarded him with a look he could no longer meet—the look of the sybil who knows what is to come, and what is to come is dark. Her glance insisted this. Let there be night.

One evening at dinner, "Nina, I wish I knew what you were—thinking," he said rather pettishly.

"Why?" she asked. "What do you mean?" She stared at him. "Why should you? Think your own thoughts."

"I believe I do," he said. But he knew as he spoke that this was not so. *Her* thoughts were thinking him.

One day when he caught sight of her in the yard, as he climbed out of his car, he experienced a feeling of actual revulsion. She looked suddenly almost ugly to him—a spry little witch, a goblin. "Stop spying on me!" he wanted to cry—though she was standing, actually, a little way off, not even observing him but looking in some other direction attentively. Later, when they were driving into town, and she began pointing out to him something about the homes they were passing, her gesturing pointer finger close to his face, he wanted suddenly to cry out, "Take your finger out of my eye!" She was too near. He couldn't breathe.

At the same time, like some spirit of faery, she eluded him. She wouldn't let him find his way back to her as she had once been.

Toward the end of the Whites' stay, Sydney proposed again a trip to St. Petersburg. "City of the walking dead," she'd heard it called—a city of old people; and she'd heard that they had balls at which, dressed like teen-agers, they danced all night long. She might like to do a story. She asked Miles whether he would drive them there the next day. But Miles had a date, with Nina, to have dinner at Rose's house. The dinner had been planned for a long time.

Sydney looked disappointed.

"Perhaps we could go in the early morning," Roger ventured.

Miles felt Nina's eyes upon him, but when he turned toward her, she had looked away.

Sydney said, "I really should see them all in the evening—out on the dance floors."

"Then why don't we go tonight?" Roger said. He added, "We'd get back awfully late, of course. We could stay over."

Sydney agreed. And they'd try to find rooms in some specially creepy place.

"Who wants to come?" Roger asked.

The Fullers felt they shouldn't.

"Nina?" asked Roger.

"No thank you," she said. Her tone was tense and haughty.

Miles turned toward her again, but still he couldn't get her eye.

Roger was joking with the Fullers. Nina cut in, "If you're going tonight, you should go right now."

Mrs. Bruce was present. "Will you stay then, Miss Wolf, and help me eat up the dinner? I've a chicken in the oven."

Nina nodded, sympathetic.

"O.K. then, children," said Sydney. "Let's be ready in twenty minutes. Roger, wear a tie. You, too," she instructed Miles.

Roger made a comic face. Miles tried not to laugh, but laughed. Then he glanced again at Nina, trying to exact some response from her before he left. But again her face did not answer him. He murmured, "See you tomorrow, Nina."

She nodded, as from a distance.

The next afternoon, Miles stepped off a bus outside of Fiddler, and walked to the house. He rapped on Nina's door but there was no answer. He changed his clothes and returned to knock again. She was still not there. He sat and waited until it was almost six. Then he started out for town.

As he approached the main dock, he caught sight of her. She was sitting on one of the rickety benches, her chin in her hand, staring across at a small fishing boat in which an elderly fisherman moved, putting things in order. She looked bunched in herself and unhappy. He recalled suddenly how she had looked to him on that first night he had joined her for dinner. He had forgotten this aspect of her. Lately she had been so fierce.

She looked up, startled to see him.

"I was waiting for you at the house," he told her. "Wasn't it at six that we were to be here?"

"Well," she said, "it's you."

He said, "I think so."

She looked all about. "Did you walk? Where's your car?"

He explained, "Sydney was anxious to see more of the place, so I left them the car."

She compressed her lips. "How did you get here, then?"

"The bus," he said.

Miles regarded her curiously. She didn't seem dressed for the occasion. She seemed even a bit dishevelled.

"Well, did you have a nice time?" she asked him. She spoke rapidly, nervously.

"Sure," he said, "it's an intriguing place, I guess. But depressing. Sydney got all warmed up, though—started taking notes. She really goes to work." He cast at her another curious glance.

She announced abruptly, "We're not going. I called it off."

Miles looked at her in astonishment.

She burst out, "I couldn't be sure you'd be back on time!"

He opened his mouth to ask "Why?," but her words rushed out, one upon the other. "I couldn't take a chance. An occasion like this is too special for Rose. When you weren't back by three, I felt I'd better stop her. She'd get meat, something festive. And she hasn't the money to throw away, all for nothing. I had an awful time trying to find her. I've walked all over the town. I have a splitting headache now." She stared him in the eye.

He had flushed deeply as she was speaking. He asked, "Why did you think I would break our engagement?"

Deflated for the moment, she just sat wearily staring at him. "Let's not talk about it," she said.

The fisherman clambered out of his boat onto the dock. He greeted Nina. "Good to see you resting your feet. Never seen such walking to and fro. Fish were talking about it."

She revived. "You! You and your talkative fish friends. Such conversations!"

He winked at her and walked on.

Miles looked sulky. "Well," he said, "then it's postponed. Till when? Tomorrow?" He sat down beside her.

"How can it be tomorrow?" She turned, angrily. "She hasn't a night off every night of the week."

"Of course," he said. "I wasn't thinking. Well, I'm sorry you called it off."

She flared again: "I knew she'd want to stay on! The idea of putting you on a bus!"

"They didn't," he informed her. "I suggested it myself."

But her words boiled up out of her. "Oh, her kind never asks for anything. People like that don't have to go asking. She knows how to put the words into your mouth. She didn't ask for the best room in the house, either. It just wouldn't occur to her to refuse it—because this is how the Fullers are trying to make their living, after all, and that room, as they said themselves in the Whites' hearing, is their big drawing card. Oh, Mrs. Bruce has their number. She's a very canny woman, I must say. 'The honored guests,' she calls them." She cried, "She knows how to be served all right. It's her one true talent."

Miles was frowning at her, disapproving. She reiterated, "I know their kind!" She suddenly inserted, "Don't think you're loved altogether for your charming self!"

His head jerked up at this, but she gave him no chance to reply. Her words flew forth from her as though they were animated beings who had at last found egress from some place of uneasy confinement. They trod upon one another to be out. "To take and take and smile and smile—that's her talent. That's her one talent. Sure, she gets down to work. She gets out that little notebook of hers and takes it all down—from everybody else. Her first novel was simply her first husband's life, all chewed up by her and spit out by her, and spun out into what some people call fine silk. He was a writer himself—originally—and it was his to write. But no. One of her most successful stories she wormed out of a friend of Roger's, who spent a year in their house." She snorted. "I wonder who told her about St. Petersburg."

"My God, Nina!" Miles said.

"You think I'm vicious," she levelled at him. "Don't worry, you have your uses, too." She mimicked, "Then we'd have a chauffeur!"

He exclaimed, "That was a joke!"

She nodded, "Oh, a person reveals himself in such a joke. I have eyes."

He shook his head.

She told him, "Look, I'm a novelist. I see these things."

He challenged her, "Nina, do you know who it was who suggested that I drive them about? You."

"Certainly," she said. "Because they were going to ask you."

He laughed then. He relaxed a little. "What a person you'd be to go to the theatre with! You'd always be speaking out what you'd know must be the next lines of the actors, if they dawdled about it."

She smiled. He had flattered her.

Miles halted. Reflecting for a moment upon his own words, it occurred to him that, these past days, he had suffered precisely from the sense of her as spectator at a play in which he performed—a spectator more sure of how the play must proceed than he, who acted in it.

He began to attempt a defense of the Whites. She listened with impatience. They had certainly been very nice to him, he ended.

She raised an eyebrow. Well, they had not been nice to her, she remarked. Such airs as that girl had put on. So careful to keep her distance.

"Hell," said Miles, "you had her terrified. She's vulnerable enough. She's not as certain as she looks." He tried to be light with Nina now. He was making his own appeal. "You *can* be terrifying," he told her, smiling.

"Oh," she said, "yes, a snake strikes out of fear, but it leaves its poison in you, all the same. Because that is its nature. I'm saying this to you for your sake," she told him.

He tried still to be light with her. "Well, I'm not walking barefoot."

"Don't be smart alec," she told him sharply.

He stiffened and was silent, sulking again. He could not contend with her.

"Oh, she knows what she is doing," Nina resumed. "She's a very knowing girl. She'll hold him, elusive as he is, don't think that she won't. He'll flirt all his life, but he'll stay with her."

Miles turned to her. "That's fine. Why do you say that to me?"

But she evaded his question. She hurried on. "I know her kind. Vulnerable, you call her. They seem vulnerable, they seem helpless. But," she cried, "everything serves their purpose. They're always in control. Everywhere you go, they are the successful ones, the fêted ones, the winners. They are the best-sellers, the ones who win prizes and grants. . . ."

He raised his head, eyeing her curiously. "Why are you so bitter about it?" he asked.

"I'm not bitter," she said, "I just say. . . ." Now she was caught up in the tirade. She couldn't stop. As she talked, she looked smaller, darker, pinched; she burned, like a small coal. She talked as another might run about, distraught. She seemed like one fleeing in confusion. And her words called up in the air between them the bogies she fled—larger-than-life creatures whom it was hopeless to think to outrun.

He interrupted again. "Why do you care? You can't be jealous."

"Of course I'm jealous!" she cried.

He stared at her. "Why? Of that kind of success?" he asked with perfect solemnity. "I don't believe it," he declared. "Your last book wasn't well reviewed, but if the people you cared about praised it, you yourself felt it was your best—what's the real difference?"

She said, "The difference is, you can't go on."

"But you do, you have," he said, easily, stubbornly.

She glared at him.

He persisted. "Seriously. Which would you rather? Who do you honestly think richer . . . ?"

She interrupted him. "Don't start quoting the Good Book at me —about the poor shall inherit the earth. I know all about it. The earth those others scrape from their boots! I've seen it, all my life. And I'm not just speaking for myself. Let's not talk about it."

But she could not stop, herself, from talking about it. Her words again spilled forth as it were of their own power. "These helpless ones you talk about," she ended, "these poor frightened people, your friends—don't worry, they leave no room for others. They grab it all. They are the takers. They are the honored guests everywhere, deferred to by everyone. By you, too," she levelled at him, "by you, too!"

Miles did not reply. He was listening, suddenly, amazed, to the words she had just been speaking. Through all these days he had been thinking of her simply as the one who had helped him to life, who had told him his fortune. He had continued to look to her to make himself clear to himself. Lately she had been providing him only with distracting riddles. Yet he had continued stubbornly to turn to her for more. Now it flicked through Miles's consciousness suddenly that she not merely witnessed events but suffered them herself

—set down, herself, in life, and regarding Fortune, where she herself was concerned, far from dispassionately. He stopped still, studying her, sober. He had forgotten, quite simply, that she, also, was human.

She asked abruptly, "Well, are you going to Key West with them?"

"To Key West with them?" he said. "No. Did you think I would?"

"I thought you might," she said. She seemed surprised.

He told her, "No, I'm not, Nina. I'll be staying right here—sorry to have to tell you."

"What do you mean by that?" she asked.

"I just mean," he said, "that I'll stay here and work."

"How does your work go?" she asked.

He said, "Every which way, thank you."

"Well," she said, "you have been bemused."

He colored. "Perhaps I have. But here we still are."

"How do you mean?" she asked sharply.

He said, "I don't mean anything. How do I know what I mean? You mix me up."

His resentment burst and he began to shout. "Damn it! I know the role you had me cast in! But you're not infallible, you know! And you might have cast me in a more becoming role—a less hopelessly helpless role!" He stormed at her. "You've put me through the damnedest week!"

She was angry, then. She was amazed. "Look," she told him, "you can't say that to me. I don't cast you. I'm not your maker. You're a big boy, aren't you? You're on your own."

He stopped still again, with nothing to answer her, as there was justice in what she was saying. She herself grew quiet, pondering *his* words. She looked tired out. And suddenly it occurred to Miles that the chief victim of the drama Nina had been watching was Nina herself—who had, in imagination, staged her own abandonment. A look of astonishment passed over his face.

Miles said, "Nina, shall we go eat some dinner?"

But she said no, she had a headache still, and didn't want any dinner. She should go home. She had some fruit in her room and that was all she wanted. She would go to bed.

He said, "I'll walk you home."

She said, "It's not necessary. You go eat your dinner."

He said, with firmness unusual for him, "I'd like to walk you home."

From one of the little boats moored along the sea wall, a heron rose as they passed, dragging up his legs after him, uttering his gagging cry. The street lamps went on. Two cars passed them along the highroad, going very fast. "Fools," she said. They walked in and out of lamplight and shadow, neither of them talking, she hurried, abstracted, and he pacing emphatically beside her, frowning to himself.

At the door of the house, she said, "No, you have to go all the way back. It's ridiculous." They both peered at each other. She said abruptly, "Well, I'm sorry, Miles. You could have stayed with them."

He said, "I'm not sorry, Nina."

"Well, goodnight," she said quickly.

The afternoon of the day on which the Whites departed, Nina looked about for Miles. She couldn't find him. She went to her room and started a letter, but she left it half finished. She looked tired to the bone—haggard-cheeked. She went outside and wandered up and down the strip of land that the fire had swept. As she paced, she stared about her. In a week's time it had already greened over. The larger pines and palms still stood up, conspicuous, ungainly, their trunks charred high off the ground and their foliage drooping above, wilted, sickly. But the ground was again in color. The palmetto, with fans faded brown, blacked at the tips, was opening out at the wrist in pleats delicate green. Nina stooped to pluck one of them.

She heard Miles's car in the yard. He got out and came over, slowly, to where she stood—he, too, staring down at his feet, at the carpet he walked upon. He took from her the palmetto fan, and turned it in his hand, smiling. He gave a slight shrug, a gesture of wonder. Her face suddenly lightened toward him. Impulsively, they kissed.

In that moment, he felt again flowing from her that intense current of sympathy that had restored him to himself in the first days of their friendship. Those days seemed real to him again. He stood musing upon the wonder of her—so two-fold a being; and for a moment she appeared again to his imagination as some ancient half-deity: one eye smiling, one eye baleful; dealing with one hand hope, with the other hand, confusion—in both opposed motions potent. If only one knew how to invoke her in her benign aspect only.

Her face clouded. She said, "I'm a wicked old woman."

He shook his head. "No."

"Yes," she said, "I haven't slept these past two nights."

He stared at her. Her face wore the curious illumination of one quite spent, and he was reminded again, with a slight shock, that she was not, after all, an impersonal force. His helplessness before her, far from being the one fact of their recent days together, was matched by her own helplessness within herself. Her suffering had been, if anything, more extreme than his. She looked to him at this moment, in fact, so very frail and tormented, that he wished with sudden vehemence that he, in his turn, had strength to give *her*. But he felt, angrily, that he hadn't.

He shook his head again. He told her, "And you were right, one is on one's own. Time to grow up—to comb my own hair."

She interrupted. "No, I'm impossible. My husband is always telling me so." She touched his shoulder, as though to confirm that he did stand there, on his own, all of one piece.

"But," she said suddenly, "do you know what he says, too? 'Who wants a life of ease?'" She smiled at him a wistful smile, bright as a child's, unregenerate.

He laughed aloud, with a kind of joy.

"Why are you laughing?" she asked.

"I don't know," he said. "I don't think there are words for it. But I love you," he told her.

An Invitation

The American girl was possessed by a curious pride, a curious expectancy. She sat on a stone outside one of the city gates of Assisi—that gate just below the church of San Francesco where the land falls abruptly away. The day was going. As it paled, the city on its mountain and the plain from which the mountain rose—of one substance always, one clay—flushed more deeply still their one color, a rosy chalk, and the light of evening, as though it were a dust thrown up by this land, hung in the air in glowing particles and dyed the air, too, this color. If I sit here long enough, the girl thought, if I sit here patiently on this stone, I, too, will be absorbed by this dye and enter the scene. She was obsessed with breaking and entering. Driven by this obsession, she had parted a week ago in Rome from Maggie, her friend, with whom she had been travelling, and had set off by herself. "To discover Italy!" Maggie had laughed, and as a matter of fact Emily had intended just that.

She had felt on the brink of discovery all week. She had been tantalized. It was such a very friendly country, it lay so open to the voyager. When she was lost and asked her way, strangers were not content to give her directions; they would seize her by the hand and lead her where she wanted to go. On buses, on trains, she would scarcely have time to settle down in her place before she found herself involved in some intense discourse. All along the way it had been the same. She had never known such friendliness. And yet those she encountered remained unknown to her. When they parted from her —at stations, at street corners, shouting warm goodbyes—they vanished utterly. She travelled in a country that was not hers. They vanished back into a life she had no knowledge of.

Yet she sat, patiently crouched on her stone, full of a stubborn expectancy. Setting out alone had gone to her head. Go alone, go unarmed, and cities will fall to you—she held this faith. Here she had been at odds, consistently, with Maggie. Go fully armed, Maggie believed; read in advance the words of other travellers about the city you are about to enter. Emily disliked to consult a map beforehand. One must begin, she thought, by wandering at random. One must turn to the map only to clarify a route one has already stumbled along, or one would never *really* read the map, never *really* break and enter the city. She even, it must be said, felt a little this way about the language of a country, and thought it somehow wrong to be letter-perfect on arrival. Come with a few phrases, she believed—the courtesies ("Thank you very much." "Excuse me, please." *"Dove gabinetto?"*) Learn from *people*. In her pride, she took this for humility. She conceived of travel rather in the terms of the fairy tales she had read in her youth. The heroine sets out in rags, and empty-handed. She is pure of heart and courteous to all she meets. (She is *simpatica*.) One

to whom she is courteous turns out, at last, to have magic powers to bestow—secrets of the place.

Not far from where she sat, four boys had been shooting pebbles from slingshots and, with shrill cries, watching them fall toward the plain. But now the boys could no longer follow with their eyes the pebbles' course. They tucked their slingshots in their belts and strolled off, arms linked. Emily rose from her stone. She was hungry. She entered the city gate and began to climb the Via Venti Settembre. As she climbed, people on the street turned to stare at her. Emily was not a beauty, she was not extraordinary of face or limb, but they stared at her because she herself stared about her in such a peculiar way—as though she did, literally, expect a door to open in a wall, a guide to signal her, smiling.

The night was warm. This was August. She had climbed a little way when she found a wine shop. Through its double doors, open to the street, a chill fragrance issued like a breath. She entered. A cask of wine had just been broached. Half a dozen townspeople were there before her, containers in hand. *"Americana,"* someone said, and nodded to her. *"Buona sera."*

"Buona sera," she replied, and smiled, looking about her intently; then, flustered, dropped her eyes.

It puzzled her a little that they spotted her so immediately for an American—even before she spoke. As a matter of fact, very nearly everything that she was wearing she had purchased here in Italy. She rather thought that she had quite changed her skin. Her sandals were from Rome, and her belt, her bag of yellow leather. Her dress had been made for her by a Roman dressmaker—cut a little high-waisted, in the Italian fashion. The label "Made in Italy" was on everything she wore. Yet, the glances informed her, *she* was labelled still: American. The proprietor wiped a glass on his apron and filled it for her. The wine was a white wine, light, dry, and of a penetrating fragrance. She gulped it quickly down. As she left, several people followed her with their eyes, laughing, saying softly, *"Americana."*

She climbed again. Above her head, a canary in one of the little cages that are hung in the streets in this town gave a trill, shaking its feathers out for the night. Emily felt a sudden exhilaration. The beauty of the evening, the wine on her empty stomach, the fact of her lonely state combined to produce in her this luxury. The taste of the wine spread from her tongue through all her limbs.

A little cart blocked her way, slung sidewise across the narrow street. A small man and a girl stood beside it. *"Gelato, signorina?"* the man asked.

"Ah, no, thank you," Emily said.

The man cocked his head at her. It was a warm night, he said (in his own tongue). "Give me an ice for the lady."

The girl opened the lid of the cart and brought out a tiny cone. "It is delicious," he said, taking it between his fingers with a very delicate gesture. "It is really delicious."

He held the ice out to Emily. She didn't want it. She wanted the taste of the wine on her tongue still, or supper. But in the fairy tales the milk cow the heroine meets on the road at the end of the day begs of her, "Milk me, dear, I am heavy." The apple tree begs of her, "Pluck my apples, dear, I am heavy." And it is the mark of the heroine that she alone—and none of her fine sisters—performs the courtesy that is asked of her. The little man obviously wanted to turn home, and his cart was heavy. Emily bought the cone. It was cherry, and sticky sweet. "It is delicious," she assured him.

He was pleased. Another? Oh, it was delicious, she said, but no thank you. The girl, she noticed, was studying her with a sweet gravity. The look was head-on, yet devoid of boldness, almost docile. Emily had met this glance before in young girls here and wondered at it. Gentleness of this variety she found a mysterious quality. The girl was a blonde Italian—though the man was very dark—a handsome girl in a faded cotton dress which was too small for her, hiked high up her slender body. I could ask them where I should eat, thought Emily. *"Scusa,"* she said to the man. "Could you tell me of a restau-

rant not too dear and not for tourists?" (She got the words out in Italian, slowly.)

The man cocked his head again, and smiled at her. Then he shrugged. "Come home with me and my daughter," he said. "Come home to my family, and we will give you dinner and we will give you a bed for the night. Then you won't have to go to a restaurant, and you won't have to go to a hotel. They are all expensive."

And here it was. The man was smiling at her, and his daughter was smiling at her, nodding. And here was her invitation. She felt herself flush. "Thank you," she said, and then repeated, "Thank you," and added, "That pleases me much." (She had mastered only the present tense.) She did have a hotel room for the night, she told him, but to come to dinner, that pleased her much.

She wouldn't need a hotel room, he said. She would stay the night with his family. They lived three kilometres from Assisi. She would ride there on the bar of his bicycle and he would bring her back into town in the morning. Emily sobered. It was necessary to stay at the hotel, she said. Her bags were at the hotel, she added. It was not convenient, perhaps, for her just to come to dinner. At the end of her statement, a question mark hovered.

The man was peering at her. "No, no!" he said. "Come to dinner. After dinner, I will bring you back into town."

Emily looked at the daughter, and the daughter nodded, her face shining. "Yes, come," she said.

The man turned the cart uphill, and his daughter took hold of it with him. They pushed it up the steep incline, Emily walking alongside them, her hand on the cart, too. Halfway up the hill, they eased it off the street into a small unlit storage room on the ground floor of a house. Inside, two bicycles glinted against the wall. The man opened the cart and leaned into it, then straightened up and handed Emily another little ice. "My name is Carlo," he told her. "My daughter's name is Francesca."

"My name is Emily," she told them, and swallowed the ice quickly, and thanked him, at which he leaned into the cart again and came out with another.

"Ah, it is enough!" she told him.

But "No—eat, without compliments," he insisted. So she swallowed that one, too.

Carlo and Francesca walked the two bicycles up the remainder of the hill. At its crest, the city's eastern gate stood up above them; beyond it, the land grew dark. Francesca mounted her bicycle, smiled at Emily, and pedalled off. Carlo straddled his bicycle and Emily slipped onto the bar, sidesaddle. Carlo gave her arm a tiny amorous pinch. Emily jumped off. She was sober again. "Ah, no! It is not possible," she said.

He just stared at her. "What is it?" he asked.

She could think of none of the Italian words most appropriate. *"Non e possibile,"* she repeated mournfully.

Carlo patted the bar. "Come," he said.

"No," she said; and added—sternly—"I am afraid."

"You are afraid?" he asked.

"Yes," said Emily.

"Don't be afraid," said Carlo.

She was silent. Beyond the arch of the gate, Francesca had stopped and was waiting for them, looking back over her shoulder. The last street light was a little distance behind them, but from the city's pale masonry was shed, still, a faint irradiance. Emily squinted at Carlo in this scant light. He was a small man. She was of average height, but he was shorter by a head than she, and of slight build. There was the look of a boy about him, and his face, too, though heavily lined—the lines those of exhaustion—was nevertheless boyish. He had a wavy, pleasant mouth. His eyes were large, glossy amber, and were fixed on her with a direct and curious regard. She hesitated. Out beyond the gate, visions flickered for her in the dark. He did not look the bully. If it came to that, she gauged herself the stronger. Besides, she thought, there is Francesca. "It pleases me much to come to dinner," Emily said, "but this other—" She shook her head. Then abruptly, she stuck out her hand at him. "Is it a promise?" she asked.

"A promise," Carlo said promptly. He pumped her hand. "Come."

She mounted the bar again, and they lurched through the gate.

Emily had seen men, women and children here—the skinny and the fat, the hale and the crippled—ride on the bar as she was doing, and had marvelled at how some of them sat there; but now she marvelled more. It was a startlingly uncomfortable seat. This road was no worse than others—a dirt road, bending sometimes uphill, sometimes downhill, past vineyards, past olive groves cloudily glimpsed—but she rode with clenched teeth. And now she felt suddenly captive, felt that she had been reckless.

With a downward rush, the bicycle turned off onto a rougher road, jolted past a huddle of small buildings, and stopped.

Carlo took her arm a moment to steady her, for she was staggering slightly. Francesca led the way, and Emily followed, stumbling up steps. Francesca held a door open for her. *"Entra,"* she said.

Inside, in a lighted room, people turned toward her in a frank amazement, and stood stock-still and staring, like deer surprised in a field—a young woman, an old granny, a small girl. "An American," Francesca whispered to them.

"My mother," said Carlo. "My wife. My younger daughter, Lucia. The signorina is called Emily," he told his family.

Emily shook all their hands. "Thank you," she said to each of them, other words eluding her.

Lucia put her hands behind her back, as though they were now strange to her. "Be comfortable, be comfortable," said the young wife. The granny pushed a straight-backed chair into the middle of the room, and Emily sat.

It was a small oblong room. The walls were roughly plastered and the floor was brick, scrubbed pale. There was one little window, set high, and cater-corner, near the door, was a low fireplace. The only furnishings were a crude table, several straight-backed chairs and a stool, a corner stand, on which were a basin and a pitcher, and a high work-stand on which stood preparations for a meal. A door into another room, which was dark, stood open. (The bedroom, she supposed—and if she had said she could stay the night, would they have slept all in the one room?)

From the dark room came a low cooing. Francesca slipped through the door and reappeared with a fat baby in her arms. "My son Beniamino," said Carlo.

The baby stared at Emily and began to roar.

The old woman giggled. "You are his first American," she said.

Emily meanwhile did feel quite like the first of her kind to be here. As she sat in the center of the room where the old lady had placed her, her pride returned to her and she began to glance about her with the eyes of one who has entered where no one before her has entered. There was no running water, she noted, and the women must do their cooking over the open fire. These simple discoveries filled her with a queer pleasure. A shelf for pots and pans ran along one wall. The shelf was decorated with newspaper, its overhanging edges scissor-cut in an intricate diamond pattern.

Carlo turned his ragged pockets inside out upon the tabletop and his wife counted the heaped, curled *lire.* The old woman crouched down on the hearth, took pine cones from a large basket, and made a fire. Inhaling the aromatic fumes that flared in the room, Emily inhaled with them the sense that now she penetrated mysteries. The old lady, still on her knees on the hearth, turned and, speaking too rapidly for Emily to understand, questioned Carlo.

"No, she must return to her hotel," he answered.

The old lady crossed the room and lifted dinner out of the baking dish in which it sat, ready for the fire, and put it in a long-handled skillet. "Then I shall fry it," she said. "The other takes too long." She held out the skillet to Emily.

"One of our rabbits," said Carlo.

The small creature lay curled upon itself in the pan, among herbs. "You understand what it is—*coniglio?*" the old lady asked, and Emily nodded.

The old lady hunched over the fire, her skinny old arm extended, holding out the skillet. The sweetish smell of rabbit filled the room. Carlo pulled a chair up beside Emily. Francesca did the same. Carlo's wife hung a pot on a hook over the fire, and then, her hands coiled in her apron, leaned against the table, smiling. Lucia walked the baby, but her eyes did not leave Emily. Lucia was small and dark, like her father, and her glance was more impudent than her sister's, and more cunning. She looked Emily up and down in detail. The grandmother, at the hearth, managed so to twist herself that she, too, was part of the circle round the girl.

A catechism began. Emily had learned, by now, to expect it. She could have spoken both the answers and the questions very nearly word for word.

"Does it please you, Italy?" asked the wife. She had the gentle look of Francesca—a tired Francesca.

"Oh, much, much," answered Emily. "It is beautiful," she told them, "and friendly." As she had not many words to speak with, she tried to give each the stress of a flight of words, and this effort involved her in a certain amount of grimacing. "Much!" she repeated, and they stared at one another, she and they, until Francesca spoke, in a voice scarcely audible.

"*Sola?*" she asked. "You are alone?"

"Yes," Emily said—for a week, for a week's *giro*. Rome to Perugia to Florence to Assisi to Rome.

"Your mama, your papa are in Rome?" asked the old woman.

"No," Emily said. "Friends."

They asked in alarm, "You have no papa and no mama? They are dead?"

"No," she said. "They are in America."

"She is alone!" exclaimed Lucia.

"My parents and also their parents are alive," Emily told them. "My father's mother is eighty," she said, smiling at the old woman. "And more lively than I am."

"Eighty," said the old woman. "Eighty! I am fifty-five."

Emily had thought her perhaps older than eighty—a dried stalk of a woman, half her teeth gone.

"And how old are you?" Lucia asked.

"Twenty-six," Emily said.

"Twenty-six!" they marvelled. "Alone!"

"I am nine," Lucia announced.

"And Francesca?"

"Twelve," whispered Francesca. Emily had thought her at least fifteen. They stared back and forth at each other.

Had she seen their churches, they asked, and had she seen the frescoes of Giotto? She replied that she had, and that they were very very beautiful. Then Carlo's wife asked, "*Cattolica?*"—was she Catholic? This was not a question, really, but an assumption. Her acquaintance made, she was found to be *simpatica*. The voices that asked this question fell always into the same little tune, which said, "We find you human. So you are a Catholic."

"No," she answered, "I am Episcopalian."

They stared.

"It is another church," she said.

They still just stared.

"It is different, but similar," she said lamely.

They looked at each other. The old lady pulled the skillet off the flame and set it on the hearth and squinted at Emily, her head on one shoulder—a hunched-up woman in a black smock that fitted her like bark, on her feet tattered sneakers, but at her ears two delicate twists of gold, a grace note. "You believe in God?" she asked cautiously.

Oh yes, said Emily, she believed in God.

"Ah good," said the grandmother. "Dinner is ready."

The table was small and they had to huddle close together—Carlo at the head, Emily on his right, Francesca next her, then the grandmother, and then Carlo's wife. A place was set for Lucia beside her mother, but she didn't sit. "She doesn't eat," said Carlo. "If she eats lunch, she doesn't eat dinner. If she eats dinner, she doesn't eat lunch. If she eats soup, she doesn't eat meat. If she eats meat, she doesn't eat soup." He cast Lucia an admiring glance, and his wife cast her a despairing one. The girl was skinnier than the grandmother. Her dress was too big for her; she had lost the belt to it and it hung on her like a pillow slip. She wandered off into the next room to put the baby to bed, reappeared and crouched on the hearth to poke at the expiring fire, then went and, tiptoe, peered out of the high window—or pretended to peer, for out of the corner of her eye, always, she watched Emily—and finally she came and stood next to her father at the table and frankly stared. The grandmother clucked at her, but she paid no attention.

The first course was a thick bean soup. Emily was very hungry and the soup was very good, and she was glad when Carlo disdained his spoon and, with both hands, picked up his cup and drank from it. She did the same. Next, Carlo carved the rabbit, and then he transferred half the animal to her plate.

"Ah, no!" she protested. "It is too much."

"You don't like rabbit!" He looked at her in distress.

Oh, yes, she said, she liked it very much.

"Ah, good, then!" he said.

But she gestured at the other plates, none of them heaped so high, and "You give me too much," she repeated.

"Ah, you don't really like rabbit!" he cried, and they all exclaimed unhappily.

Oh, she liked it very, very, very much, Emily assured them and, to convince them, ate. Francesca filled her glass with wine and Carlo told her, "Drink, drink!", so she drank. And Francesca filled the glass again, saying, "Drink! Please!", and Carlo piled onto her plate what was left of the rabbit.

"No, no!" she protested again, but "Ah, it isn't good, then?" they all cried, and she assured them that it was very, very good, and made gestures to convey this, said "Mmmm" and rolled her eyes up, and— to convince them—ate.

When she had cleaned her plate, Carlo grinned and wiped his mouth and pushed back his chair. And Emily spread her hands wide and said to each one of them, "Thank you."

The rabbit and the wine, the summer night, the fire's incense, and simply the fact of her entry into this house, made her feel now a little giddy.

Carlo rose and vanished into the other room. He returned with a large alarm clock ticking in his hand. He set it on the table and faced it toward Emily. The hands pointed to five minutes of ten. "It is time to take you home," he said. "You can take Francesca's bicycle. She can get a ride in the morning." Francesca nodded eagerly.

So Emily stood up and tried again to say thank you. She stuck out her hand to each one of them, and opened her mouth, hoping for more words than "Thank you very much," but none would come, so she repeated, *"Grazie, grazie—molto, molto,"* gesturing, to give the words stress. Carlo was holding the door open, and she stepped out, looking back, still gesturing, still hoping for a little rush of eloquence.

The terrace outside seemed to be unevenly paved, because her feet couldn't find the level. She kept shifting them, there in the dark, trying to stand up straight—thinking, Am I drunk? She had forgotten that she had approached the house by a flight of stone steps, and she suddenly sprawled out violently along the ground. The family came running down the steps after her, with cries of alarm. She got to her feet. She said, "It is nothing!" Her wind was knocked out of her and her right arm stung her sharply, but she could stand, and nothing seemed to be broken. Their cries subsided.

"Come, then," Carlo said. Francesca held the bicycle for Emily to mount. Her eyes had adjusted to the darkness, and she checked herself again and she knew that she wasn't seriously hurt, but as she sat there astride the bicycle, trying to balance it, she felt suddenly altogether helpless, and fallen from joy. She asked herself what she was doing there in the night, sitting astride a bicycle, among these alarmed strangers. She had the queer sensation of awakening abruptly far from home, as one awakens sometimes in dreams, set down somewhere one has never been before, absurdly and without transition. She hadn't ridden a bicycle since she was sixteen. She wasn't sure that she still could. But "Come," said Carlo, and she called "Goodbye!" and followed him.

Emily's bicycle wobbled from one side of the road to the other for a while. Then she straightened it out. At the main road, Carlo let her pass him. Then he wheeled up alongside her and reached over and gave her cheek a tiny pinch.

"So here I am," she said to herself listlessly. "Here I am." She shook her head and said "No!" emphatically, and he dropped back, then wheeled up alongside her again and, squinting at her mischievously, made kissing sounds upon the air. The moment that she had felt bold to cope with had come round to her, but meanwhile she had lost belief in the entire venture. Even as it was happening the moment seemed remote, and the means to cope with it more remote still.

He whispered, "Stop a minute, Emily. Here, stop a little."

She said, "No," again and decided, I will simply keep pedalling and hope that I have breath enough. *"Non e buono*—it's not good," she scolded him and, concentrating upon pedalling, she managed to pull ahead of him.

"Emily, stop a little!" he called. So she stood up (remembering that this was how to put on speed) and, bent over, pumping hard, reached the top of the first hill.

She really expected him to overtake her easily, for he made this trip every day, after all. "But my legs are longer than his," she told herself hopefully. The stretch was downhill now for a way and she used it to catch her breath. The next hill was easier for her, and then there was a long, gentle downgrade. She sprinted here and, looking back over her shoulder, she was surprised to find that she had left Carlo far behind.

She heard him crying after her. His voice reached her in a sudden shrill gust from over the crest of the hill she had just descended, and she slowed down, because there was nothing of invitation in the call, now, but only alarm. She wondered, What can be the matter with him? And suddenly she realized, He thinks I am stealing the bicycle!

The road passed some houses here, and a group of people were on the road, taking an evening turn, so she felt safe to stop. He came pedalling frantically down the slope, crying out, "Where are you going?" and pulled up, gasping. He stared at her. She stared back. They were both aghast. "Where are you going with the bicycle?" he cried.

"I am going to my hotel," she said.

"And why are you going so fast?" he said.

She dismounted, and he dismounted, and each, holding awkwardly still to his bicycle, poked his head forward in the half light to scan the other's face. Carlo threw out his free hand. "I brought you home with me. I brought you to my family. We made you welcome. We fed you. And now you run away with my daughter's bicycle," he cried. "Now you run away with my daughter's bicycle."

"No—*Senta*," she said. "Listen!" She was flushing at his words, but at the same time she felt like relaxing into laughter. "Believe," she said, finding that word. "Believe."

He cocked his head. She turned to the bicycle and gestured as if spurning it. "No, no," she said. Then "Yes," she said, "you were good to me. You were very good to me. All the family. And thank you! Thank you! *But*"—she put everything into that word—"*Ma*," throwing out *her* free hand, then raising her eyebrows at him—"this other thing." She shook her head at him. "*Cattiva*—bad." She suddenly remembered this word. "I was afraid," she said. She repeated, "*Paura* —fear." The walkers were alongside them now, and hushed their voices and turned about to look at them.

"*Sono ignorante*," Carlo said, "I am an ignorant man. If it had pleased you, it would have pleased me. But I am not a man of violence."

Then Emily did truly have nothing to say, because she was ashamed. Go unarmed, and the place will fall to you—she had boasted this faith. But now the fact was uncovered to her that she merely travelled blind.

She said, "I believe it." She repeated, "I believe it now. *Scusa*— forgive me." She said, "Listen"—speaking painstakingly—"*una ragazza ha sempre paura. Necessità.* A girl always has fear. It is necessary." She asked him, "Do you understand?"

He smiled in astonishment, and she said, "Excuse me. Do you understand?"

Again she stuck out her hand at him. He looked at it and grabbed it and shook it. They both laughed. "*Allora*," he said, and they mounted their bicycles again and, side by side, rode the rest of the way to the city.

At the gate of the city, Carlo said, "Would you have a drink with me, to say goodbye?" She said that she would.

He put Francesca's bicycle in the storage room, and they went to a bar down the street. He had a glass of beer and she had a glass of sparkling water, for she felt she had had enough of intoxicants for that night. He became distressed at the sight of her arm, which was a little bloody from the fall, so at his request the bartender poured some gin along it, against an infection. They touched glasses, Carlo downed his beer, and she thanked him again. She asked him to write his name and address in her notebook, which he did with a little diffi-culty, and they peered at each other once more, still looking surprised, each at the other. Then they said good night. Outside, he turned uphill and she turned downhill toward her hotel.

The streets were empty, and Emily's feet made a lot of noise on the cobblestones. The canary that had sung for her earlier awoke as she passed and hopped across his cage once, but sounded no note. A white cat with one broken ear walked with her the second half of the way home. She got her key from the drowsing man at the hotel desk and climbed the stairs to her room.

The water had been turned off, or had failed, so she crawled into bed without bathing, the dust of her fall still on her. Her right arm was stiff, and one finger was quite painful. Her body felt as though it were someone else's body, not her own, and she was again dispirited, as she had been after her fall down the steps. A group of young men passed below her window and stopped to have an argument. Their voices rose clear in the summer air, but though they were not talking very fast, not a single word they spoke sounded familiar to her. She had had it happen before, when she was tired out: the language suddenly would go over her head like a great wave, and though she had been making some progress in it, it would be only gibberish to her. And she felt again, What am I doing here in this country not my own? Her pride was quite gone out of her breast. She lay this way a long while before she dropped off to sleep.

However, in the morning she felt differently. On the bus that took her down the hill to the railroad station, she recognised an English girl who had arrived on the same train with her the day before. They smiled at each other, and the English girl crossed and sat down next to Emily. The English girl had spent the night, she told her, at the house kept by nuns up on the hill. The sisters had been very kind to her, she said, in spite of the fact that she herself was no Catholic. "Rather not. I'm a bit of an atheist, as a matter of fact." And where had Emily gone?

So Emily recounted her adventure, with some abridgements, but telling of the ride through the darkness on the stranger's bicycle, of the rabbit cooked by the old woman over the fire built of pine cones. "And leaving, I fell downstairs and broke my finger, I think." She held it out. It was very swollen.

"Gosh!" said the girl. "And they asked you into their home?"

They both stared at the bruised finger as though it must possess certain magic properties gained from that evening; and they turned to gaze back up at the ancient city upon its ancient hill.

"Well, you really discovered the town," said the English girl.

And Emily began to feel again that she had discovered it.

Death and the
Old Woman

The old woman was dying. This was the doctor's opinion; it was not the old woman's opinion. Nor were her family able to believe in it. She had been declared dying before, and she had already accomplished ninety-seven years. Let it be gently said that her family could not believe in it because for too many years they had been looking forward to it. For all these years she had lived not merely her own life but, without restraint, as many other lives as possible, and those of her family, of course, had most tempted her. So they had hungered for the day when their lives would be their own at last. Obsessed with that day, they had long since ceased to be able to imagine it.

Florence Rouse lay in the local hospital eyeing her nurse from one of those beds with sides that look like cages. Back at the house she had left, her son and his wife waited, immobile as she; unable to stir or to think. Her son lay with his leg in a cast. He had fallen on an icy street the week before. "A slip in time," his mother had remarked. "Now he doesn't have to visit me." His wife could not visit easily, either. She was having the terrible migraine headaches that often plagued her. "And that's just as well," said Mrs. Rouse. "She has never been able to address me directly. So what would she have done? Propped up his photograph between us, I suppose. 'Dear, is your mother feeling any better today?'"

It was Caroline, her granddaughter, who visited. For this too Mrs. Rouse had tart words: "Might as well have sent the cat." For her granddaughter had been ignoring her latest advice and so she had been elaborately ignoring her granddaughter. The young woman had been afraid, even, that her grandmother might have the nurse turn her away. But she did let her visit. Caroline moved between home and hospital in agitation.

She too had wished for the old woman's death. It was difficult for her not to wish it when her parents wished it so much. As a child, she had wished it for their sakes; older, she often found herself wish-

ing it for her grandmother's sake—the life she led was such a bitter one. But the thought of it now filled her also with terror. A passage from the Bible ran through her head, distorted to a new sense for her: "If a man abide not in [the vine], he is cast forth as a branch, and is withered. . . ." Her terror was lest her grandmother, in dying, be cast forth out of life utterly. Before this time, death had never seemed to her dismaying. Those whom she had known to die had seemed to her to live on after death, as vivid sometimes in memory as in life. "Abide in me and I in you. . . ." The generations formed together one vine. Of course by the vine the Bible meant Christ and his church; but the words had come to hold for her an unorthodox meaning. Now it was hardly that her grandmother, after death, might be forgotten. Her presence among them had been, as far back as she could remember, the central fact of that household. But the manner in which she had lived among them had been a peculiar one. A visitor to the house had once asked, "Do you live here with your son?" "No,

I don't live here," she had stated sourly, and when her son had exploded, "Mother, how absurd! You've been living here with us some fifteen years," "No, I don't live here," she had repeated. There was a more than literal sense in which her statement was quite accurate, for in their hearts both she and they furiously denied the arrangement. She could never really live where she did not reign absolutely; and they, for their part, had cultivated over the years a careful amnesia where she was concerned: there were times, when she wasn't actually speaking—indeed there were times when she was—when her son and her daughter-in-law seemed almost successfully to be pretending that she wasn't there. And so it wasn't that she might be forgotten; but her memory would be resisted as her presence had been. Caroline would make her memory welcome; for she had come, over the years, to love her—that is, to hate her and to love her at the same time; and she had come to cherish the fact that she was descended from her. But would her grandmother accept this particular welcome? Or might she not declare of this too: "No, I do not live here"?

The two of them had always been at odds. And the more Caroline had come to love her, the truer this had become. For she was a greedy old woman and she asked all or nothing. She would if she could make Caroline her creature. If you love me, you will do my will. Caroline had learned to be elusive. Her grandmother had set this fact to rhyme:

> *There is a young lady named Carrie*
> *Who is so very wary*
> *She never sits down*
> *But fidgets around*
> *Ready to leave at my query.*

Caroline could hear now, in imagination, the old woman's challenge: "Here I lie. And you want to stroll in and, standing first on one leg, then on another—no time to sit down—give me your blessing: Then off again about your business. I don't need it."

Nevertheless Caroline was obsessed with one purpose: to prevent her grandmother from dying in loneliness. The old woman would seek, probably, to disdain her love—any love not given on her own terms. But somehow she must be persuaded to accept it.

This war of love could not have reached its crisis at a less auspicious time. For Caroline and her grandmother had just had a quarrel. Caroline needed a job and Mrs. Rouse had urged her to try for one in radio. "You say you want to be a poet. There's your audience! Get your foot in that door!" She had an old friend she wanted her to see at a local radio station. But Caroline had applied instead for a teaching fellowship on the West Coast. Her grandmother had argued with her that her parents needed her at home, but Caroline, disagreeing, had sent the application in anyway. Since then the old woman had not been speaking with her or acknowledging her presence when she entered the room.

For the past three nights, before the ambulance was ordered, Caroline had been her nurse. Her grandmother had refused to acknowledge her presence even through those hours. She had let her needs be known to her by signs, without speaking to her—her long finger pointing or her eyes flashing at what it was she wanted: the red pill or the yellow pill, milk, more ice in the milk, more whiskey (a medicine she had prescribed for herself), or the pillows banked up behind her (for by now she must sleep upright or wake in a coughing fit)—she had given her haughty signals in the air as though it were the objects themselves she summoned, and her granddaughter did not exist. Caroline meanwhile had played a role as stubborn. She had tried to keep up the pretense that her grandmother's wrath did not exist—replying to her always as though she had made a courteous request. Each had sustained her own part without breaking, though by the time the ambulance came, the morning after the third night, each showed the strain.

By the third night, the struggle between them had become outlandish. The old woman had often to get into the bathroom that opened off her room. The first nights she had staggered a little, in danger of falling; but by the third night she was too weak to rise from the bed by herself; and still she would not allow her granddaughter to put hands upon her to help her. With blazing eye and palms upraised she forbade her to interfere. She sat on the edge of the bed, her puffed old feet swung round to the floor, but not quite able to get herself up onto them, her breast heaving, her face flushed with the effort, and her eyes wild, as she flopped back each time helpless. But as Caroline put out her hands simply to be ready to catch her if she should start to fall, she commanded, "Keep your hands by your sides!"

It took her twenty minutes to heave herself up and then to inch the short distance to the toilet—onto which she fell awkwardly; but she accomplished it by herself—Caroline standing there, marvelling and exasperated, her hands by her sides. And she attempted a second trip on her own, wavering this time in the middle of the floor, so sick that she no longer even knew quite how to begin to move her feet—or which foot was which—but from the springs of her being summoning up the will. And she managed again to flop herself down on the toilet, and managed again to rise. But on her way back this time she had to grab hold of Caroline. They stood there, clasped, in the middle of the room, her granddaughter holding her up and she half swooning, but even now not acknowledging that Caroline helped her, her flesh simply not acknowledging the contact. And Caroline, exerting all her strength—for her grandmother was a big woman—eased her to the bed and down upon it. Propped there on the bed's edge, her grandmother looked up at her and then—in helplessness or in vengefulness?—began to slip, eyeing Caroline, who hung on, straining to prevent it, straining to somehow fling her back onto the bed, the old woman with her eye fixed on her speaking at last a second time as she settled on the floor: "Well done!"

Caroline had run for her mother and then—the two of them could not lift her—had run for a neighbor just up the hill. For him Mrs. Rouse had a crooked smile and a quip: "Quietly now. My poor son needs his sleep."

At the first sight of her grandmother caged in the hospital bed, Caroline halted in the doorway. Stripped down to the hospital smock, her blackrimmed glasses removed and the yellowing switch which she stacked on top of her own now meagre hair, the mask of powder and rouge gone, and gone from about her the camouflage of her own room —lying there quite like an animal in a trap, snatched abruptly from its daily life—she looked both more sick and more potent, more pitiful and more impregnable. There she is! thought Caroline, There she is!—staring as one does at an animal behind bars; in grief that he should be caught so, and on guard, not really believing that he can be held.

Mrs. Rouse, when she sighted her granddaughter standing in the doorway, awestruck, her arms full of flowers, cast one cold look in her direction and turned her head away. Caroline gave her flowers to the nurse ("I am Miss Kelly," said the young nurse). Then she approached the bed—drawing on patience in a motion almost visible, the carefully calm face, calm voice, of the past three nights. She delivered her messages of love from home. (These were invented. Her parents had watched her leave for the hospital, as though in a trance, wordless.) Her grandmother did not look at her. "Dad feels so badly that he can't visit," Caroline repeated herself. The nurse, returning with the flowers in a vase, held them out for her patient to see. Star-

ing past them, the old woman inquired of the air, "Your father—does the doctor hold out a little hope for him?" Miss Kelly looked from her to Caroline in surprise. She was a sweet-faced young woman, with a small turned-up nose. The old woman informed her, "He slipped on the ice. I wasn't there to hold him up." The nurse's look of wonder provoked her to further animation. "His students will all be in to scribble on his cast, I suppose. Carry him over here to me," she demanded with sudden ferocity; "I'll sign my name to him. What a piece of work is my son." The young nurse, embarrassed, turned to put the vase of flowers on the bureau. She stepped back to take her patient's pulse. "Now," said the old woman, "my granddaughter will have somewhere to appear. She's a poet but the world doesn't know it." Caroline, embarrassed in her turn, moved to the bureau to ease the roses in the vase a little. "Which way is North, which way is South?" cried the old woman. She still addressed the bewildered nurse, but it was Caroline for whom her words were chosen. She was quoting now from one of her granddaughter's poems. This was a pastime with her. "What are the words that blow out of my mouth?" she chanted.

She began to cough. "Hush, you're trying to talk too much, gran!" Miss Kelly told her, holding her up. Caroline had started toward her, but her grandmother had stopped her with one glance. The fit subsided. The nurse wiped her forehead, shiny with sweat. "My Park Avenue cough," whispered the old woman.

Caroline decided that she had better not take a seat. She was still half expecting her grandmother to dismiss her. She drew near the bedside again. "Is there anything I forgot to pack for you that you'd like me to bring?" With this question she did at last gain the old woman's direct attention.

"You may bring me a bottle of whiskey," she said. "What I have isn't going to last very long." The little vial of whiskey she always carried with her stood on the bedside table.

Caroline hesitated, looking toward the nurse. "Will the doctor let her have it?" she asked.

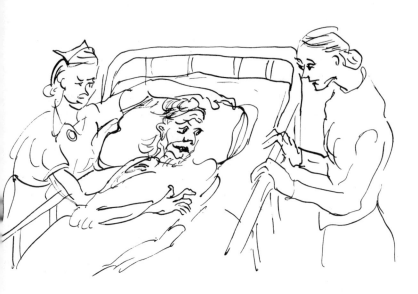

"I'll see him . . ." the nurse began.

But the old woman's voice cut hers down. Miss Kelly stared, for this was a voice she had not heard from the patient. It was the voice Mrs. Rouse summoned for the telephone (half believing still that it was the voice by itself which must pierce the distances), it was the voice she used on servants, the voice by which she made her wishes known and clear—each syllable given an accent, e-nun-ci-at-ed: "You may bring me a bottle of whiskey," she told her granddaughter. "*Get it?*" The last two words were spat.

The nurse stared again. Caroline turned her head aside—anger against her grandmother suddenly flooding her. On her way out, she whispered, "I'll be back tomorrow."

Back home, her parents asked no questions, but greeted her with asking, non-asking eyes. "Did you have any trouble on the road?" her father wondered; "it must have been slippery down near the river."

"No, it wasn't bad," she answered. "She's comfortable now," she told them. "The hospital bed makes all the difference. They can keep it jacked up high for her. She seemed quite peppy, really." Their eyes expressed, in spite of themselves, alarm.

As soon as she could, she sought out her grandmother's room. She was restless to approach her again, and to enter this room was to do so. She felt quite hopeless. It used to be the sport of emperors, she mused, to watch two gladiators who had been given mismatched weapons—one a sword and shield, one a trident and a net. She and her grandmother were contestants as unevenly matched. Her grandmother held sword and shield and trident too, she thought; and she simply a many-times-mended net. Too often her own anger tore it. How ever could she catch the old woman? How could she avoid entangling merely her own self in love's knots? She stood there, wary as in her grandmother's presence, and cast her eyes about the room.

In ancient Egypt, when a member of royalty was buried, there would be buried with him the likenesses of food, drink, servants, pets, jewels—all that the deceased had enjoyed while living, so that they could continue to serve his will. The excavation of one of these tombs would reveal to the digger an image of the royal state. So it was here. For Mrs. Rouse, taking up her residence in this room fifteen years back, and entering it as though she entered her tomb, had dragged in with her the memories of *her* pleasure.

Above the door, over Caroline's head, heavy-hung the great Conte-Galli hors d'oeuvres plate. "Many famous hands have plucked olives out of my Conte-Galli." Mrs. Rouse's list of these great tended to extend back even into days it was not likely she had seen. "It's not everyone can say that she has had an interesting conversation with Disraeli." "Ha, the parties I have given!" Her nostrils would flare as though breathing again that finer air, the incense of days that were her own. "Before I lived in a cupboard. Like old Mother Hubbard."

The room was of decent enough dimensions, but it *was* crowded, with the heavy Italian pieces she had dragged in upon the early

American ones with which her daughter-in-law had furnished it. Caught in the many-winged mirror of her large dressing table, a piece like great aunt Bissell's maple desk did look a little skimpy, and to accentuate this fact she had poised on its narrow top the giant samovar that had served her "multitudes." Her carved arm chair elbowed other pieces into corners. And her gallery of pictures took up every inch of wall. Looking down into this room from elaborate frames were those who had done her bidding—or those who would have done it if they had not been mad or doomed.

Her husband, Frederick, leaned from his gilt laurel wreath frame, elegant and mild, his fist full of paint brushes. His money had enabled her to give those parties which had then set him on the verge of Artistic Success (or so she declared, to whom success was a matter always of moving in among the right people; from that, all would follow). But death had intruded. Casting about for help now, Caroline's eyes glanced upon him. Should she invoke his name? For *he* had loved her—apparently had done her pleasure readily. Or had he, in dying, fled her the only way he knew how?

From a larger still more elaborate frame looked forth her son, the second Frederick. Staring at the picture of her father, Caroline stopped invoking others in the name of love; for she knew that her father was unable to feel love for his mother any more. She remembered with a pang his remark some years before when he had been about to undergo a serious operation. He had told a friend (who had repeated it to Caroline), "Don't worry about me, please; I am determined to outlive my mother." The picture of her father was a self-portrait, executed in the days when he still faithfully carried out his mother's wishes: he at his easel, smiling out at her, and from the studio wall behind him, the carefully copied self-portrait of his painter father, smiling out at *him*. Caroline could still recall the voices that had been raised, when her grandmother first moved in with them, over whether or not this picture was to hang in their living room. It never had. But of course anyone who entered the house was led by the hand into the old woman's room to view it. "He had a remarkable talent. But one does not light a candle and set it under a Bissell."

Alice Bissell's face—her mother's—was absent from this gallery. Possibly, had he never met her, her father *would* still have been living out the life the portrait imagined—swept round Europe in the wake of his mother's parties. (Portraits would be his fortune! She would surround him with subjects! Now they must return to America, for she had endless connections there to exploit. And she herself would "dabble a little in oil—the Texas kind.") But the return home had brought him face to face with "Miss Bissell-body"; and under her influence he had resigned pretensions as a painter and become the teacher he had long wanted to be. It was at this time that there had occurred those tantrums and those wild connivings on her grandmother's part which neither her father nor mother would ever forget or forgive. Her mother, in her temperate fashion, matched Florence Rouse in energy. She had the advantage, besides, of finding Mrs. Rouse a little vulgar. She had stood up to her. And so, finally, had Frederick. When her grandmother took to tampering with the mails, her mother had been confident enough to know it and to circumvent it. When her grandmother took to falling in swoons upon the floor, her mother had found it in her to step across her prostrate body—at which, of course, the body had revived; and her father too (as her mother told the story) had finally stood up on his feet. Teaching was Frederick Rouse's proper profession, and over the years, his mother had been compelled to note the reputation that he had gained for himself. But his success was not in terms she could understand. Look at the house that they must live in—she must live in (her own income squandered finally on her adventures in oil). They could not even afford a full-time servant. She had had six "in service."

From the walls stared forth those who were to have restored her to fortune, those in her "debt," one of whom, some day, would surely repay that debt in gold. "They'd not have gone far without that push

I gave them!" There grinned forth her husband's cousin, the banker —for whom she had found the right house and "furnished it with everything he needed—including the right wife. 'You'll never lack for anything while I'm alive,' he told me. That very week he died in an automobile crash." "But someone may yet repay me," she would muse —year after year.

Caroline's own likeness looked back at her there. She had, at any rate, not been removed from the wall. Her grandmother had hung round the frame the poetry medal she had won at high school. But there had been nothing so shiny to show since. Poor high-stepping old woman, thought her granddaughter—to see her blood, as she must think, thinned down to this.

The room held the scent of her grandmother still. Her mother, she saw, had flung the window wide open, to let in air, but the scent hung there impervious—and summoned her now tangibly before her granddaughter, witty, disdainful. The dominant note was her cologne, one that smelled somehow of incense. She may want that, Caroline thought; I didn't pack it. She stepped to the dressing table to get the bottle.

On the label of the bottle was a bright design showing Eve and the serpent. The picture suddenly recalled to her with a shock a dream her mother had told her about, two years before. Her grandmother had travelled to the hospital then, too, pronounced dying. Two weeks later she had returned. The morning after her return, Caroline's mother had told her, puzzling, "I had the strangest nightmare last night, Carrie. I dreamed that someone had killed a poisonous snake in the garden—cut it in half. But then the two parts of its body joined together again and it crawled into the house." Caroline had not interpreted the dream to her mother.

Dear poisonous but splendid old woman, she thought; dear persisting old woman—do I think that I can contend with you? And she paused, also, to wonder: is she, even now, really dying?

Over her grandmother's bed hung the Rouse coat of arms: a

moated castle with a wind-stiff banner, lettered: *"J'endure pour durer."*

The next afternoon when she mounted the hospital steps again, she had in her arms a number of bundles for her grandmother. She held them to her gingerly, picking her way from the car across the somewhat icy winter ground. She was carrying the bottle of whiskey her grandmother had demanded (the doctor had given his O.K.); also the bottle of cologne. And on an impulse she had added from her grandmother's desk a small photograph of her grandfather. She had wanted an ally, a charm.

Once inside the door of her grandmother's room, she felt abruptly self-conscious. But she took the photograph to her grandmother's side. "I thought you might like to have this here." The old woman looked at it without comment. She asked, "Did you bring my whiskey?" When Caroline answered, "Yes," "Put some more whiskey in my milk," the old woman told the nurse.

Caroline set the photograph of her grandfather on the bureau, under the flowers, his mild eyes turned upon his widow. How much slighter he was than she, she mused. Her grandmother was not fat and not taller than is ordinary, but she was large of frame. She had a very large head, sunk a little into her shoulders, hunchbacked with age and with coiled up power. She is handsomer down than when up and about, thought Caroline, staring at her as the nurse fed her whiskey in milk through a glass straw. Up and about, with her wig on and her rouge, and hung with beads, and her silvertipped cane flicking before her, she was marvellous to see. No one whom Caroline knew made so complete an effect—and this still, though her dresses tended to be a little shabby, now that she could no longer see to sew, or see not to drop food on herself. (Caroline, hanging things up for her these past days, had been startled to note what rags they were. When she had had them on, she so invested them with her own pride.) Trapped out, she was marvellous. But there was something a little grotesque in the vision, too. She was a figure out of Punch and Judy. (She had just this effect, Caroline noticed, on the man who came round to the house to do odd jobs. She had seen him once, when the old woman appeared at the door, eager for gossip, pick up a broom— without knowing what he was doing—and strum it like a guitar, as though she might go into a zany dance for him. And her grand-mother, as a matter of fact, to her amazement, had done a brief jig for him.) Lying there as she was now, out of costume, she was finer looking than one would have supposed; and her face, for all its wicked thrust, was delicately fashioned. But it was a bold face always, with its great arch of nose, its gash of mouth and unusually long upper lip. Her ears were quite large and long. Her chin was stubborn, jutting. Her eyes glanced out, blackbrown, quick, immense, from be-hind these prominences. Her hands were quick as her eyes and as imperative. Even now, hump-veined and gnarled, they moved above the coverlet, electric.

Caroline had been designed less boldly. On her, the big nose seemed a little out of scale. She had not the ears to match it, or the upper lip. She had also her mother's paler coloration. She was taller than her grandmother but slighter—hunchbacked, a little, not with power but with hesitancy. "Always frowning, always musing, always wondering, always weighing," her grandmother would chant. Still, you could see that she was the old woman's kin. The total effect here, too, was a stubborn one.

The nurse, returning the glass to its tray, reached under the bed-clothes to make some check on her patient. Mrs. Rouse reared up, come to life: "Are you mauling me again? Last night," she informed Caroline, "two demons attacked me; but I fought them off."

"The doctor wanted us to catheterize her," Miss Kelly whispered to Caroline.

The old woman swung her glance upon her: "I'll resist you all, little lady—to the end." She informed her granddaughter, "The night nurse left me for two or three hours. They were having a party down the hall. All the birds and the beasts were there. See that it's taken off the bill."

She had another sudden violent coughing fit. Caroline knew better, this time, than to run to her. Miss Kelly held her up. As her choking subsided, she intoned ferociously, "Her sis-is-ter us-est to boos-es-ter." As Miss Kelly shot Caroline a sidelong look, it suddenly occurred to her: They think she is delirious! Her snatches of limericks and tongue-twisters, bits of Shakespeare and the Bible—this is a speech they have not encountered before. And again it occurred to her: she may not be dying at all; for when they think they know her, they do not.

She sat for a moment, but then stood up. At her gesture of settling down she could feel her grandmother grow restive. She had not been there very long when a neighbor arrived. The neighbor was a great admirer of Mrs. Rouse's and had counted on her often to enliven her teas. Mrs. Rouse tended to make fun of this woman, but when she stepped to the bedside now, she gripped both her hands in her own and chanted loudly for Caroline's ears, "She is the tree upon which the fruit of my heart is growing!" She added, "Now you can go along, Carrie." Caroline, before leaving, stopped by her side and touched her hand. Her grandmother pretended not to notice.

Miss Kelly walked to the stairs with Caroline. "What did the doctor say this morning?" Caroline asked.

Miss Kelly told her, "He doesn't really understand why she is alive."

Ha, thought Caroline. She told the nurse, "She isn't delirious, you know. That's the way she always talks."

Miss Kelly nodded. Then she added, "She's frightened now. When we're alone, she wants to hold my hand. She keeps telling me, over and over, 'I'm so afraid.' "

And Caroline left, shaken. Then she *is* dying, she believed at last—if she herself thinks so. And even so she will not let me draw near; turns, in her terror, not to me but to a complete stranger. She thought: how deeply angry at me she must be, if even the fact of approaching death can not dissolve that anger. To look at this appalled Caroline—and for a moment roused her own anger again, in response. She despises my love, she thought, for I am a failure in her eyes; always turning from her counsel, I turn in that gesture from grace.

Nevertheless, she thought, I must insist that love. She thought this with an edge of anger still. And conscious, suddenly, that it was an incongruous element in such an impulse, she asked herself: Could the real truth be that her grandmother turned from her simply because she had never made her love for her sufficiently believable? Yes, she loved her, but it had been easy enough to put her out of mind, too. And she had been ready, after all, to leave for California— though it could well have meant that she would never see the old woman alive again. Perhaps when her grandmother had argued that Caroline's parents needed her, she had really meant: *I* need you—and had felt abandoned. Caroline left, this day, despairing and in terror.

Home, her father asked, "Carrie, should you maybe have chains on the car?"

Her mother still lay in her room with the curtains drawn, her face haggard.

When Caroline arrived at the hospital the next afternoon, she stepped to the bed and then stood staring down at her grandmother. She was asleep, uneasily, her mouth wide open (the nurse had removed her teeth), her head flung back against the pillows and her arms out by her sides, her hands in the gesture of grasping. And her breathing had changed. It sounded like some small gasping engine that is breaking down. This discord was punctuated by a queer note like the note of a whistle under water. And Caroline, staring, heard above these sounds a further sound, quite distinct, as of a fly buzzing in circles. This sound was so precise that for a moment she looked for the insect there in the air above her grandmother's dishevelled head. But there was none. It is Death, she thought, circling above her. But she will not let it settle; she will not let it alight. Her body lay stiffened against it, her brow knotted against it, and with her breath she blew it from her.

Caroline stood there still, staring. If the day before had made real for her her grandmother's fear of dying, now for the first time death itself was real to her.

Miss Kelly edged a chair under her and she sat. How does one pray? Caroline wondered.

Miss Kelly whispered, "Are you all right?"

Caroline whispered back, "Yes."

She had leaned her head for a moment against the side bars of her grandmother's bed. How does one pray? she wondered. You are loved! she began to pray, you are loved! But the old woman's rigid sleeping form denied it. She will hold me off as she holds off death, thought Caroline—with her last fierce breath. She recalled as a young girl hearing her father challenge his mother: "Mother, you'll have to give in this once!", but she: "I am what I am! I am what I am!" But one cannot stand out in this lonely way throughout eternity, thought Caroline—in terror now at her grandmother's terror. How does one pray? she wondered.

Outside, it began to snow. Caroline, lifting her eyes to the window, saw the quiet flakes falling beyond the glass. She prayed: Fall on her, dissolve her, reconcile her.

Meanwhile a fly seemed to circle in the air above her grandmother's head, and the droning note to call forth, as it will, summer in all its fullness.

Miss Kelly sat with a copy of the *Reader's Digest* in her lap, sometimes turning the pages surreptitiously, sometimes watching the old woman and Caroline. At one point she got up and tapped Caroline on the shoulder and gave her a glass of water.

The day began to go, as Caroline sat hunched there by the bed-

side. The snow fell more lightly. Mrs. Rouse stirred but did not wake. Her breast rose and fell more easily, and the discord of her breathing subsided. Her hands released whatever it was she had grasped in her dream. It was as though within her sleep she slept.

"It is the first time she has rested like this," said Miss Kelly in a whisper.

It was dark when the old woman woke. She opened her eyes suddenly and smiled at Caroline. And she spoke in a blurred mild voice: "I just had the sweetest sleep."

Caroline whispered to her, "It's late, but I wanted to wait and say hello. And I'll come again."

Her grandmother stretched out her hands to her. "Yes, come again tomorrow," she said.

Caroline drove the miles home, over the whitened roads, slow-motion, her heart in turmoil, thinking: then love, after all, does find its way.

Home, she found that her mother had staggered up from her bed and made dinner for her. Before sitting down to it, Caroline made an excuse to slip into her grandmother's room. There, in light quick motions, she straightened the pillows on the bed, the jumbled objects on the bureau, her hands performing, without her thinking, any gesture, any gesture of love.

Later, sitting in silence with her parents, she remembered suddenly a look her grandmother had given her across the table one Thanksgiving Day. Some of the Bissells had been there, her mother's brother and his family. The Bissells were always very stiff with Mrs. Rouse, for they knew something of the family history. The three children had contracted the hostility of their parents and were barely polite to her. Watching the conversation pass over and around the old woman, who sat grim and haughty, not even bothering to listen to what was said, Caroline had tried catching her eye at intervals and smiling at her, calling casual remarks across the table to her. Glancing at her toward the end of the meal, she had found the old woman staring at her, and suddenly her grandmother had mouthed, surprisingly: "I-love-you." And I, you.

The next morning the doctor phoned to say that there was no need now for Caroline to visit, unless she wanted to, for Mrs. Rouse was in a coma and could not wake from it. But Caroline went back just to sit by her again.

The doctor was wrong. Mrs. Rouse was awake. When Caroline came in, Miss Kelly had her propped up high and she was having her whiskey in milk. The nurse still wore on her face the look of surprise that had appeared on it when Mrs. Rouse woke. The old woman pushed the glass away and spoke.

The nurse asked her, "What is it, gran?" Though she had broken out of her sleep, she was not disentangled from it. Her speech was confused. "Don't worry about it, gran," said the nurse.

The old woman's eyes flicked from one to the other of them. Her cheeks grew red. And from some terrible depth of her she summoned out of anger enunciation: "This-isn't-cold-enough!"

Miss Kelly stepped quickly for ice.

"You'd better go," the old woman told her granddaughter, getting out the words barely—"I can't talk."

"You don't have to talk," Caroline told her. "I'll just sit here, just to be with you."

Her grandmother shot her a baleful look.

The old woman sank back after her drink and lay there, panting. And sleep seemed to come over her, then, but she shook it from her. Her hands moved upon the coverlet, as though seeking something to which to cling, to keep from going under. Caroline began to try to pray again.

Her grandmother started to hiss like a cat. For as she lay there, Death formed before her eyes. She hissed it off. It formed more clearly. She screamed. Caroline rose to her feet, but her grandmother turned from her to Miss Kelly on the other side of the bed. She grabbed at Miss Kelly's hand. The nurse wiped the sweat from her forehead with a towel: "What's the matter, gran?"

Caroline sat again. She tried to pray, but her spirit trembled too hard. Her grandmother sank into sleep and came up out of it again; sank into sleep and came up out of it, gasping. Her eyes widened as Death, in the air above her, moved in too close. She screamed.

Caroline jumped to her feet and, not thinking, bent and kissed her grandmother's cheek.

The old woman turned round on her, hissing, "Why did you do that?"

Caroline, aghast, whispered back, "I love you."

The old woman turned her head aside. And soon she said to Miss Kelly, "Tell my favorite granddaughter to go. She tires me."

She couldn't go home yet. Mrs. Rouse's nephew and his wife had wired that they were driving over this afternoon to see her. They lived some distance away. She had better wait, to meet them, she thought. She went downstairs, to wait in the entrance hall. A young farmer was sitting on the bench there, waiting for news of his daughter in the operating room. He kept rubbing his eyes, as though to wake in some other place, and raising his nose to sniff at the antiseptic air—bad weather. Down the corridor, two nurses were in a fit of giggles over a whispered exchange of news.

She sat for a while, across from the troubled man, and then got up and paced up and down. She felt: What have I been trying to do? I have just been annoying her, in my own delirium. It is not my prayers she wants, and not my insisted love. She wants, very simply, for as long as possible, not to have to know that she is dying. I have been reminding her of it and that is all that I have accomplished. She knows enough to send me away. She remembered stepping to her grandmother's side with the photograph of her husband—from which she had turned away her eyes. All she really wanted me to bring of course was whiskey—life. She could hear suddenly, loud in her ear, her grandmother's voice chanting a verse that was a favorite of hers:

> *Oh what a thing is love*
> *It cometh from above*
> *And settleth like a dove*
> *On some*
> *But some it never hits*
> *Except to give them fits*
> *And take away their wits*
> *Hohum!*

God forgive me, she felt; I have lost my wits, and been impertinent in the word's full sense.

Her relatives arrived. The nephew was an economist, a tall good-natured man with dimples at the corners of his eyes. He and his wife were her grandmother's most cordial relatives. They had always appreciated her as a dramatic figure, and they had never lived very near her for very long.

She tried to prepare them for how their aunt might be; and she stood in the door as they went in. The two of them drew near the bed and the old woman turned and stared at them. They murmured their greetings. From the door, Caroline could see that they were taken aback. Mrs. Rouse held out her hands to them vaguely. "My nephew," she tried to say to the nurse—she gestured in the air—"has often been recommended to the government." Her nephew and his wife strained their heads forward, trying to understand her, but they couldn't decipher her speech. The wife still clutched some flowers they had brought. Miss Kelly took them from her now and she thanked her. The old woman wet her lips with her tongue. She was trying to speak again. She stared at her nephew. "I'm writing a book," she told him. (But he couldn't make out the words.) "It's called 'I'm afraid now, I'm afraid now.' It's going to sell all around Caroline's beautiful literature." The nephew tried to smile at her. He told her, "You'll feel better very soon, Aunt Flo." And they both stood there, awe-struck. "You'd better go now," the old woman mouthed, slowly. They did not understand her. Caroline whispered from the door, this time, what it was that she had said.

The two of them followed her back to the house, to speak a few words with her mother and father, but they turned around soon for home. "They were so good to come," said her mother, "and so good to go." Caroline retired to bed early. She was still shaken. Her grandmother's final words had further humbled her. Such wit, in the middle of terror! And in the middle of terror, such disdain! She was shaken by pride, herself, in her grandmother's pride, however fatal; and by a kind of ribald despair of her own strength, matched against her. She *is* what she is, she thought, and who am I to have thought to succour her? At the end of this day, she had quite resigned her action.

Nevertheless when she woke the next day, her purpose had returned. She discovered it to her own surprise—that she had not actually resigned it.

This morning again the doctor had reported that her grandmother was in a final coma. Again she had broken out of that sleep. But her speech today was quite gone. She could articulate now only the one word, "Whiskey." "It's all she asks for now," Miss Kelly told Caroline. She asked for it incessantly. She pulled at it in long hungering sips, as though it were air and she coming up from under. Sometimes she struggled to speak. But it was no longer the nurse or Caroline whom she addressed—except to call for whiskey. It was Death Himself. Her eyes no longer seemed to hold any other image. Her tongue managed, her lips out-thrusting it: "I–I–I–I–" Can she get no further with the sentence? Caroline wondered. Or is this, in fact, the all of it—her two words, two remaining words, the same: whiskey (life)—I—I live still, am what I am, here I am.

Though she had had from her today no hostile glance, because no glance at all, Caroline drew near warily. She sat not too close, with her chair by the window. She was careful, even, at first, not to gaze at her grandmother too openly, lean out of her eyes too far. And it was in this manner that she prayed—so quietly within herself, at such a shy distance, that the air about her could not be troubled by it.

The next day, too, the doctor told Caroline that her grandmother would not wake again; and the day after that, and the day after that. Each afternoon, she came to sit by her, all the same, and each afternoon she found her wakeful still. Her grandmother lay heavily now, her limbs passively washed by the tides of sleep, but her head still heaved above the flood, sipping life—her nostrils flared with it and her mouth gasping it in, drawing it in, her upper lip desperately out-thrust. It is as though she hangs on by that great lip alone, thought Caroline—a great tortoise, clinging to this floating thing, this life.

Her grandmother no longer shied from her now. Perhaps she no longer recognised her. Her eyes were alight, but what they watched was no longer within that room. As Caroline slowly drew her chair in closer, there shaped before her eyes as well the hovering images of Death. She prayed: Death, she is loved. Put a value on her. But sometimes she simply sat and stared, in awe. Here, she felt, are two adversaries who are matched: Death and my grandmother.

As the old woman no longer sent her away, she sat there now throughout the long afternoons.

Meanwhile, outside the window, the countryside was locked in winter. The snow had turned to ice, and every branch and twig lay in an icy casing. Fretting in that vise, the trees shifted in the winds with the sound of leather creaking. At day's end, when the declining sun caught in its pink shine all this glass, a Springtime was simulated, so brilliant that it hurt the eyes. "Melt away, melt away," her mother tried chanting at it from her window.

The ninth day was Sunday, and Caroline reached the hospital before noon. The morning nurse, Mrs. Beman, was still on. She was an older woman, stout and chatty. Mr. Peters had been in earlier, she reported, but he had stayed only a moment. Mrs. Rouse had told her about Mr. Peters when she could still speak. "He wrote a book, she said. Said she'd lend it to me but that I should burn it when I was finished with it. She wouldn't want it found among her belongings. Said it was filthy." Caroline laughed, amazed. To the end, she thought. Peters was her father's close friend, a young instructor in literature.

"Well, it's a love story," she told Mrs. Beman. " 'Filthy' doesn't really describe it. How is she now?" she whispered.

"The same," the nurse answered. "It's a marvel. The doctor says she's full of . . ."

"Shhh!" mouthed Caroline, gesturing toward her grandmother.

"Ah, she can't hear us, dear," the nurse told her. "She's under. And when she's awake, she's only half awake. She doesn't recognise us."

Caroline insisted, "But you can't be sure, can you?"

"Oh, she can't hear us, dear," the nurse repeated.

But Caroline was thinking: If her familiar senses have faded, perhaps she is aware in some new way.

Mrs. Beman said, "If you're here now, I'll just duck down for a sandwich."

And Caroline told her of course, and sat, relieved to have her go. When Mrs. Beman came back, she avoided her eye, not to have to talk again.

Her grandmother had not roused to ask for whiskey in some time now. The nurse stepped over to take her pulse. She looked over at Caroline: "Her pulse is as strong as mine." She said it with a kind of surprised outrage. Ha, thought Caroline, they do not know her. Her grandmother lay there now, breathing as profoundly as a sleeping baby, mouth open, one hand across her breast. The old woman's words came back to her suddenly from that time two years before when she had visited this hospital. Nurses had been scarce and the first night Caroline had sat up with her—for then, too, everybody had thought that she lay dying. As day broke, her grandmother had whispered to her, "I will remember what you did for me this night as long as I live"—and Caroline had been struck with awe at the accent she gave those words, the vista that had opened out of years unwinding one from another endlessly. Not many weeks ago, she had watched her readying herself to go out for tea, peer into her great mirror, cock her peaked black felt hat at an angle, then wink at her image, "Hello, you old witch!" Staring at her sleeping grandmother, "Hello, you old witch," Caroline breathed. The great lip sucked in the air, drew it in. I think, Caroline mused, that she has found the very Source of life; she lies there like a baby at its very breast, pulling at it, peaceful, and is immortal now, cannot die. And musing this, she felt the pride of the old woman running in her own veins. Then, very suddenly, her grandmother's breathing changed. The nurse stepped to her side again. Suddenly her breathing was rapid, broken—as though she panted above a stream from which she could not drink fast enough.

"Why, I think she's going," said Mrs. Beman. She said to Caroline, "Go to the desk, dear, and ask them to send the house doctor to this room."

Caroline ran down the corridor, to give her message, thinking: I must get back. When she got back, her grandmother was breathing normally again.

The house doctor arrived. She was short and redfaced. She went about her duties rather as though she had been rudely dared to. She did not bother to nod to Caroline. As she pulled the hospital gown down ungently from Mrs. Rouse's old breasts and placed her stethoscope, "Be gentle!" Caroline wanted to cry, "She's alive still"—adding, "She will outlive you all!"

The doctor declared to the nurse, "There's nothing really that's worth doing. Her doctor didn't expect her to pull through?"

"No," said Mrs. Beman.

"Ah well." She left.

Then it began again, the rapid lapping at the stream. Mrs. Beman stepped to one side of her, and Caroline to the other, the old woman's body sitting up now, crouched strangely, the nurse holding her. Caroline saw her grandmother's face wrinkle up, slow-motion, as though to cry. It crinkled up as children's faces crinkle up when something they want is taken from them—and before they have learned to dissemble crying, and stiffen chin, mouth, eyes against it. She saw it crinkle all up from chin to forehead—as it was taken from her.

Mrs. Beman said, "She's dead."

The house doctor returned. Again, without ceremony, she pulled the hospital smock down over the flat old breasts, to place her stethoscope. She looked at her watch, a large one. "Three past three," she said, as the station master might note the arrival of a train. Mrs. Beman jotted it on her chart. The doctor turned on her heel and left. Miss Kelly had entered, and stood near the door, in unbelief. Mrs. Beman patted Caroline's arm. "Are you all right, dear?" She told her,

"If you should want me, I'll just be down the hall."

Caroline still stood close to the bed. She felt: I mustn't move yet. She felt: If they come back and try to take her away, I shall bark at them like a dog: Keep off.

Miss Kelly stood watching her, with an inquiring look. Seeing the look, Caroline asked her, "May I stay here a little while?"

"Of course," said Miss Kelly, and she asked her, "Would you like me to pack up her things for you?"

Miss Kelly began gathering up the old woman's things: the bed jackets Caroline had packed for her, but which she had never worn; her cologne; her comb and brush, her hairpins and the yellowing wig; the photograph of Mr. Rouse.

"There's a little whiskey left in the bottle," said Miss Kelly. "Shall I pack that?"

"No," Caroline said, "I guess not." Spill that to the ground, she thought. To the Gods.

She drew a chair suddenly close to the bed, and sitting, placed her hand upon her grandmother's shoulder. The shoulder was still living to the touch. She stared at her grandmother shyly. Her face looked very fine in death—bold, beautiful, and without malice now. Her eyes had been shut, and the nurse had closed her mouth, too, but it had fallen open again—more beautiful so, reaching out still for life, the whole thrust of the face toward life. As she sat there now, Caroline's heart slowly stopped its cry of *no no no no,* which had begun at the sight of her grandmother's face wrinkling up as though to cry. Sitting here by her now it slowly occurred to her that she had witnessed an affirmation to marvel at: that her grandmother at ninety-seven should put still such a value on life that she could cry like a baby to have it taken from her. She felt, suddenly, hope again, clear in her: she *will* persist—was sure of it, suddenly, that her grandmother's life would not be snuffed out; feeling: Death must surely value less those who run to him uncombative; and thinking: if she found human love unmanageable, to life, simply, in itself, she did give her heart.

As she stared at her, her grandmother's tongue stirred suddenly in her mouth.

"Her tongue!" she whispered at Miss Kelly. "She's not dead!"

Miss Kelly, starting, whispered back, "No, no! It's just that as she relaxes—"

Miss Kelly looked at her as though she should leave now. But Caroline sat there thinking: I mustn't leave yet. For there are some whom one might leave and no sacrilege, but surely *her* spirit clings still to its flesh. Except that she was not thinking, but only sitting, waiting—as, under her hand, the old woman's life circled to its stand-still in her veins.

Miss Kelly shut Mrs. Rouse's suitcase and set it by the door. She said, "I'll say goodbye."

Caroline thanked her and the nurse left. And she sat on.

Her grandmother's shoulder was cold under Caroline's hand. She stood up, gazing down at her. Now, she thought, it does not house you. Now you no longer cling. And she stood there, blank. Still she did not go away. She stood there looking down at her grandmother, her hands by her sides, not knowing what she waited for. Nevertheless, I just stand here for you, she felt, not thought.

Suddenly, out of blankness, it seemed to her that from far off there was a terrible out-reaching to her, a crying out. Without thinking, she held out her arms in the air, as though to answer: Yes, yes! Don't be afraid! And you do live in me.

She heard footsteps approaching the door. Quickly—before anyone could come in—she leaned and pressed upon her grandmother's cold cheek the kiss the old woman had not let her give before.

An Illness

Look how her pencil goes!" cries the maid at the pension, and she stands with arched neck, on tiptoe, trying to watch her own portrait appearing in Marianna's sketchbook. "Dios! Is that Hove?"

"You're supposed to stand still," Marianna tells her.

Marianna is less concentrated upon the portrait than Hove is. Her hand moves with an absent-minded skill. She is really waiting for it to be time to go into town for the mail.

She won't find the letter that she wants, and she knows it. But every morning at this hour a ghostly hope springs up in her. A half a year ago her lover left her, to marry another woman. Marianna hasn't been able to pick up her life again without him. In spite of herself, she is hoping to be able to go on by finding that he wants to return to her.

Her reasoning self knows very well that he will not come back. She has exerted herself to understand why he left and to her surprise she has been able to see why. He needed a wife, and she never was quite that to him, though they lived together for six years. She had been wary of becoming *just* his wife—afraid of being submerged by household duties; of finding that his work (he was a painter too) counted, between them, for more than hers. As it turned out, she tells herself, it was he who had always to be remembering *her* work; she had to be reassured regularly of his respect for her. One day he met a woman who wanted only to be married to him. He agonized for a while and refused to abandon Marianna, but in the end he went.

She thinks she can understand his going. Her rational self resigns him. But between her understanding and her suffering is a break; the two don't touch. She puts herself in his place and she understands. But then she is recalled to herself and quite as though she had not just understood, the cry rises in her: But why? Why did you leave me?—followed by the whisper: He will come back. There may be a letter today. And so it is this imaginary letter she is really scanning, in secret—not Hove, who begins to beg, "Give me short curly hair today, like yours, Señorita, to see how it would look on me." And Hove begins to laugh, with her hand over her mouth, and laughs so hard that she sits down on the floor.

There is half an hour before lunch and Marianna starts out for the post office. The pension lies at the edge of the Mexican town, where fields and wooded hills begin. The street she takes is uncobbled, and badly pitted; she picks her way. She is small and erect and walks with a rapid stiff-legged walk, her shoulders moving in a pronounced way. It is a vivid sunny day. Above the adobe garden wall of the first house she passes nod small bright sunflowers, and blackbirds whistle among them. She jerks up her head, sees the birds, and smiles vaguely. A young man jolts by on a mule, his bouncing body hitting the mule's back, slap, slap. In her path, two large white butterflies blow here and there, like paper scraps. Marianna startles slightly at every movement in the street. Her glances are distracted; like the butterflies—which blow backwards and against her skirt as the boy on muleback passes—they settle nowhere. She is carefully not thinking too precisely of the letter she hopes for, because if she does, she will stop believing in it, and so she lets her attention wander, and it takes to itself now this impression and now that, but lightly, not to disperse within her that vague anticipation which makes her at this hour almost, but not quite, gay.

As she approaches a certain poor-looking house, a small boy darts out from its doorway—he is dressed in patched trousers and a dirty flapping little shirt, barefoot. Each day when she goes by at this hour, he jumps forward, and executes for her the same dance—eyeing her fixedly and flirtatiously. He hops up and down, in place, moving his shoulders violently. The dance is his imitation of her walk. This fact hasn't occurred to Marianna, but his hectic motions in her honor entertain and touch her. She waves her hand at him: *"Adios."* "Yoss!" he explodes in a whisper, *"Goot* bye!" After she has walked on, she looks back over her shoulder. He is standing on the same spot still,

waiting for her to turn, and as she does, like a wound toy he repeats his dance.

The street makes a turn and becomes cobbled. The shops begin. Bright coarse Indian blankets hang in the doorways and leather purses from the ceilings. A glance brings the shopkeeper forth: *"Venga, venga,* come right in." In some shops, men are tooling leather. Their hands are diligent and move at their tasks, but their eyes are elsewhere—upon the street, to mark what passes. One of the leather workers tries to catch Marianna's eye, his brows arched at her. But Marianna's eyes are straight ahead of her now. The post office is at the end of this street.

At the post office there is no letter. Her spirits desert her, replaced by dullness.

It is lunch time. At this pension, everyone eats at one long table. The elderly Dutch woman who runs the place presides—a stooped anxious woman, always worrying about her servants: "Naughty children! I can't turn my back!" The other boarders, all Americans, are two young vacationing couples and Lou, an older woman, widowed a few years before, who has ever since been seeing what the world is like. Lou is late to lunch; she has been away overnight on an expedition. Marianna has not interested herself in either of the couples. And neither couple is interested in Marianna—though one couple would have been if she had let them. The look on her face of abstraction and suffering has frightened them off. The first time they bubbled over about themselves to Marianna, she forgot to listen to what they were saying. When they got all through telling her about their day in Oaxaca, "Have you been to Oaxaca?" she asked them.

The Dutch woman is telling now about the young man who arrived last evening and went on his way this morning—headed "somewhere faraway," but he wasn't sure where.

"You had a talk with him, didn't you, Miss Stone?"

Marianna looks vague. She had breakfast with him. He came in for his breakfast before she finished hers, and after she left, the Dutch woman joined him for a second cup of coffee. Here is how the young man's breakfast with Marianna went:

He sat down directly opposite her—giving her a tentative bright smile, and then, ducking his head, settling into the chair in a hurry, as though it were the one empty place on a bus. He had a look eager and afflicted. He twitched up his brow as though he couldn't get his eyes open wide enough. His "Good morning" asked a question: Will you welcome me?

Marianna felt instantly a kind of tenderness for him. And she thought: He is unhappy too, for some reason.

The young man noticed the tender look she gave him. The color rose in his cheeks and after he had swallowed his fruit juice he began:

"Are you here for long? Or just passing through too?"

She said, "I'm here for a few weeks, I guess." She began to think, "I wonder where I am going from here."

He volunteered, "I've been travelling for two weeks, but I'm not sure where I'm headed."

She smiled at him and nodded. But at her smile, instead of telling her more, he suddenly felt unable to. Her smile was gentle and full of feeling. It indicated: yes, I know; I too. But it was quite lacking in curiosity. It gave him a sense that he was hardly sitting there at all. She was sitting there, and in some fashion he was a part of her feelings; but as a person with a history distinct from hers, he remained invisible. They exchanged a few more words—about the jam (they wondered what it was made of), about the weather (they wondered what it would be)—but for the most part they were silent. He sat hypnotised by her, watching her eat her toast, drink her coffee with a queer delicate greediness, as though she asked instant nourishment of the meal: give me back life! Then Marianna excused herself, with a smile at him so sweet and yet so vague that he stared after her. And the Dutch woman joined him.

"He told me all about himself," said the Dutch woman. Now Marianna is startled; she stares at the Dutch woman. For the first time it occurs to her that she hadn't thought to wonder about the young man; and it occurs to her that he had been eager to present himself. For the Dutch woman is not one to draw people out.

He is just back from a year's service in Korea, she tells them. He's sure that he's going to be called up again, for another war, and he's looking for some place where, in the time out they'll let him have, he can forget what's coming and live along as though it weren't so—some place where one can make-believe. He's asked her what Peru is like. It's remarkable the sympathy he's provoked with his story. Bus drivers have put him up for the night. Complete strangers have fed him. He's hardly had to spend a cent yet of the money he's saved.

Marianna suddenly feels listless and guilty. She asks herself why, but is too listless to answer herself.

There is a rumpus of dogs in the courtyard. Lou has returned. Hove runs headlong through the patio, her slippers flapping. "Hove, don't run, please," calls the Dutch woman. Lou hurries in, shouting back over her shoulder, to the guide, thank-you's, instructions for to-morrow. The two dogs of the household dash before her, and Hove and another servant skip in her wake, clutching saddle bags, baskets, thermos bottles. "If you drop those, I'll beat you," Lou turns as she strides and threatens. They bend double with laughter—"*Oh, la señorita!*"—and scramble for her room.

Everybody at table sits up, a little more alive. All feel themselves, suddenly, taken notice of. "I'm too hungry to wash," Lou tells them. As she sits, the two dogs crowd each other at her elbow, wanting to be petted. "Later," she says, "all right then, hello; hello." She lifts a paw of each and kisses it—"there, there!" She is a sturdy white-haired woman, with a broad vivid face, very blue eyes. She wears rough boots and canvas riding breeches, but a flowered blouse. On her wrist a bracelet jangles, and on her fingers are two immense rings. "What a damn-hell beautiful ride I had!" She begins to eat ravenously. "Just don't watch me," she begs, "I want to talk, but I don't want to stop eating." She begins to tell them of where she's been. She interrupts herself to ask what has happened here in her absence. Suddenly she strips off her bracelet and her rings. They get in the way of eating. She sets them on the table beside her, laughs, and thrusts one of the rings at Marianna—"Feel!" The ring is hot. "Lord, what a ride!"

Marianna holds the ring in her hand, thinking, hungrily: Ring, warm me. Pass to me some of her zest.

Lunch is over and Marianna retires to her room. She sits on her bed and looks through her recent sketches. They are pallid work and she can see it; they communicate nothing of this country. Anger against Ralph suddenly takes hold of her. She accuses him: You have left me this way—no longer capable. You have left me for dead! She feels a doubled anger that she must admit to this. She has always hated Plato's image of the creature sliced down the middle, only half a creature until it finds its other half again. But it's true, she thinks now; and she can't forgive Ralph for having brought her to thinking so. But as she begins to abuse him, she is filled with horror at herself, and further desolation. For she loves him. She stretches out on her bed, exhausted.

She begins to blame his wife, but to think of her torments Marianna. Now she hears again Ralph's stammered explanations and suddenly compassion for him floods her. She thinks, in a rush and with relief: I do forgive you. But in the motion she longs after him all over again. She sees him before her—gesturing widely, too emphatically, with his large-jointed hands. And the remembered sense of his presence is dismayingly more real than the sense of her own presence in this unfamiliar room.

She jumps up. She decides to go out for a long walk and look about her hard, to forget him.

She leaves the house. Walking fast, and staring about her, she starts through the village. She chooses an unaccustomed way and as she hurries along, she strains to take note of everything, commands all her senses to report to her. The town smells of woodsmoke, of coffee, of flowering bushes, of mud. A cock is crowing from the east; an ass is braying in paroxysm from the west. The red tile roofs of the town are scintillant in the clear bright light. The sky is windless and a church set on a hill is cocooned in a delicate grey motionless puff of cloud, the hill under it very green.

Marianna stares about her, trying with each observation that she manages to secure the scene through which she travels, to nail it there on either side of her. But even as she walks and stares, there leaps up in her a conversation with herself. She tries not to attend, but she cannot help it. Soon she doesn't see where she walks.

These conversations are, monotonously, always the same, and they are in themselves monotonous. "But you said—", she exclaims in herself. Some phrase out of the past starts up before her, something that he once said. "But you said once that I was necessary to you." The argument never progresses very much farther. But it occupies a long interval of time. She utters to herself that declaration he made. But as his words conclude, they stand denied by the present moment in which she is. And so she utters them again, as though by doing so she can make them of one piece with this present—alter it. She utters them again and again. Or she rewrites the past—calls up a scene that never was so. He is about to leave her and something she might have done or said holds him there. As this imagined scene ends, the vague impression that she does still hold him ends with it. She calls up the scene again; fashions words, gestures; as they fade, fashions them again.

She has walked to the outskirts of the town. The road here crosses a little bridge, above a narrow hurrying chocolate river, and then forks. It is the crossroads out of town. Sick with fancies, Marianna sighs and looks up. The sky has changed without her noticing. There is a wind now, high up, and the piled clouds are dislimbing rapidly—unravelling downward and sliding west. She stands, hesitating whether to go on or turn back. An old woman in a streaked brown ragged shawl is crossing the bridge, coming toward her. She peers at Marianna. *"Niña, rova?"* ("Dear, are you wandering?") she inquires. The question startles Marianna. Yes, she thinks, I wander.

She thinks: How can this happen over and over? This is how she has travelled through Mexico. She had started out on the trip as she started out on her walk this afternoon, boarding each bus along the way with the resolution to look about her and forget herself. The wheels of the bus no sooner began to turn than her fantasies leapt up between her and the new country slipping past her—those other, imagined scenes flicking again before her eyes, always the same worn film, jerky footage. Her memory of Mexico is in fragments: a glimpse of a town suddenly, when the bus stops, or a glimpse of open plain (where have the three men sprung from, standing by the side of the road, sombreros joyfully lifted?). Or: at a burst of laughter from the driver, she looks out. An old man on muleback has decided to race with the bus. He trot-trots just ahead of it, with his skinny heels giving the mule's sides a jerking flurry of kicks. In the distance she recognizes with a start Popocatepetel, its volcano top reared out of mist as if out of the air itself. She wonders for how many miles it has been visible. What country lies between the glimpses she catches, she couldn't say. She remembers her trip as children remember voyages taken at night. At intervals they wake for moments in their parents' arms and stare out at scenes that are strange to them. Each time they wake, they wonder for a moment: How did I get here?

Marianna mumbles a greeting to the old woman and hurries by. She is dismayed. Only two days before, out walking, and dreaming in the same fashion, she looked down suddenly at the ground where a rustling slender snake of a pale color slid across her path. She had almost stepped on it. She started violently at that encounter too and —violently—thought: Yes, remind me that I am walking in my sleep! But as many times as she is reminded, she falls into her stupor again.

At the other end of the bridge, by the side of the road, three little boys are playing marbles. There is a rough stone bench there and on an impulse Marianna goes and sits down on the bench among them.

"*Buenos días!*" she greets the children.

They answer explosively, "*Dias!*"

They exchange among each other swift secret glances and continue the game. They are of varying ages—the oldest perhaps twelve (he has the faint beginnings of a moustache), the youngest about six—all three raggedly dressed and barefoot. The youngest, when he gets up, limps and has a large dirty rag tied round one toe. This child has the habit of shuddering convulsively every now and then.

"Are you cold?" Marianna asks him.

"He does that," they tell him. *"Malhecho!"* they laugh. ("He is badly made.")

The most adept at their game is a thin boy with a very narrow head and small sooty black eyes pushed deep under his brow. He makes a particularly good shot and jerks up his head, with a quick sniffing intake of breath, but without smiling.

Marianna exclaims "Aha!"

"Aha!" they parrot her, and glance at her with amusement.

And now the marbles begin to roll against her shoe every other shot or so. Two of the children pretend not to notice, but the youngest can't keep from looking up at her each time. So one of these times she reaches out and, in the traditional fashion, "steals" his nose. Out of the corner of her eye she sees the oldest boy, with a smile, imitating the gesture to the sooty-eyed one. He has translated it into another traditional gesture: a fig to you.

Abruptly she asks the children, "Is that the road to the ruins?" She points to a path that runs off across a corn field and up into the hills. Somewhere near here an ancient temple has been excavated.

"Yes, the temple of the tiger!" They jump to their feet. "The stone tiger! We'll take you!"

She is surprised that they want to and suddenly she feels a little spirited, a little bit awake.

"Vámonos!" she declares—"Come!"

"What are your names?" she asks, as they set out.

"Roberto"—they point to the oldest, a round-faced boy with trousers too long for him: the cuffs are muddy. "Manuel"—the sooty-eyed one taps himself lightly above his heart. Manuel points at the youngest: "George Washingtone." They eye her. She wonders whether it is a joke on her or whether it can really be his name; smiles and tries to look as though she is not in this doubt.

By the side of the path they take, a delicate red and orange wildflower is growing that looks like a small snapdragon. She points at it. "What kind of flower is that?"

"It's poisonous!" Manuel declares dramatically, "poisonous!" He picks up a stick and knocks a number of the heads from their stalks.

George Washingtone pounces upon the severed blossoms. He manages to stick one to each of his eyelids, tilting his head back to balance them there. Then he does a limping dance before Marianna, humping his shoulders and lifting his knees, a carnival figure.

Marianna laughs. She feels her heart lightening.

The path begins to climb the hill and to grow rutted and stony. George Washingtone takes Marianna's hand to assist her. Manuel promptly takes her other hand. They walk with an air of festivity.

Suddenly the two boys let go her hands and all of them scatter like rabbits into the brush. *"Tigre! Tigre!"* they shrill, as they vanish, casting backward looks at her that spell out "Terror." She is left alone on the path. She should act scared, she supposes, but she doesn't feel quite that playful. She decides that the simplest thing is to hide for a moment, herself; so she steps behind a large oak tree there by the path. She leans against the tree to get her breath.

At the foot of this hill, in the corn field they have passed through, a farmer is breaking off ripe corn. The rustling sound of it reaches her where she stands. At the far end of the field she notices an adobe hut, a little blue smoke curling from the vent below its roof. She watches the curl of smoke diffuse itself above the hut into the afternoon air and suddenly self-pity overwhelms her again. She thinks: Why am I here? Why am I homeless?

The children reappear upon the path.

"Is it far now?" she asks.

"Not far!" they shout. They take hold of her hands again. She lets them lead her on, but she no longer feels adventurous. The children are quick to notice the difference in her and they vary their sport. If she is not responsive, the game is now to see how much can go unnoticed. They hurry her along. She wonders: Are they helping me or hindering me? She seems always to be putting her feet into the worst ruts. She releases her hands from theirs. They scamper beside her, laughing. After a minute or so, their laughter becomes bated, tremulous, and she becomes aware of an odd other sound. As they trot along beside her, they are peeing into the air before them.

Now I am a victim for them, she thinks; they are mocking me—and she stops abruptly.

"That's stupid!" she tells them, and she turns about and starts back down the path.

They come trotting after.

She tries to pretend to ignore them and quickens her pace, but they keep alongside of her. She begins to stumble and she notices that her shoelace has broken. She squats down on a stone to repair it. George Washingtone promptly kneels at her feet.

"No, thank you," she tells him, but with a little shrug at her he extracts the broken lace and, painstakingly, knots the two pieces together. Then he begins to lace up the shoe again. But she suddenly finds that she is really angry, snatches the laces out of his hand and—forgetting even to address them in Spanish—bursts out, "Go away! All of you!"

They stare at her, and they go.

Marianna finishes tying up her shoe. And then she continues to sit there glumly on the stone. She is astonished at herself now, and ashamed, for they had hardly deserved that outburst. Their mischief had not been grave and their gallantry had been as real as their mischief. She sees that her anger had really been because she had felt out of control of the situation; and she sees too that if she had not been abstracted, this needn't have been so.

Suddenly reproaches against Ralph rise in her again: You have left me helpless. She tells herself: No, I must stop this. Here I am, beginning it all over again. It is absurd. She thinks: Help me, help me—but helplessly asks this of him: Help me, then, somehow to forgive you and to take hold of my life again without you.

Then the poison of her bitterness starts to run through her once more and to numb her faculties. She feels with horror: Here is the taste of it in my mouth again. And she hurries home, trying to think of nothing, trying not to attend to the fantasies that once more shape themselves about her like an enchanted hedge.

Back at the pension, as she is crossing the patio, headed for her room, she encounters Lou. Lou is sitting out there in a camp chair, rubbing her riding boots with neats-foot oil. The two dogs are with her, getting in the way of her work, and she keeps pushing them off: "Get away, nuisance!" "Where did you walk?" she asks. They chat for a moment, and as Marianna is leaving, Lou gives her suddenly a long measured look. She is wondering: Should I ask her to come along on my next trip? At the ranch I'll visit there are people she'd probably like very much. But scanning Marianna's face, she decides abruptly: No, she'd weigh me down. She has troubles and she's heavy with them. I'd have to carry us both along. Marianna notices the look and notices its abrupt withdrawal, and she is puzzled and disturbed, but too abstracted to know how to question herself about it. She returns to her room.

She sits down on her bed. Outside the small high window, the sunflowers in the walled garden across the way nod slightly, their yellow heads dipping upon their furry stalks. A blackbird hops from one flower to another, shaking the heads more emphatically. Marianna gets up and walks to the window and stands staring out. And as someone else might yearn, with sudden force, to be some particular place where he is not, Marianna—staring at the dipping flowers, the hopping bird, the scene which is right there and yet, for her, curiously remote—suddenly prays with vehemence: Let me be really here, here in this place and this time where I am.

The Rattler

Jack Hanna sat on the sea wall, "fishing"—in his city pants and city shirt, sneakers and wilted white golfing hat; an old man with thin mouth and small beaked nose, with flat belly and chest, with that compact look that makes one feel: there is nothing here to spare, every bit of this is he. He had baited his line and dropped it in the water, but his eyes were shut. He had begun to sit out the hours of the day here, and he always held out his fishing pole in front of him, because he didn't believe in doing nothing; but the line wavered unregarded in the current, and his thoughts wavered within him, as slack.

Hanna had come down to Florida two months before. For years he had lived in a town in upstate New York, employed as caretaker and gardener for a men's club, and living alone, a widower, in a furnished room around the corner. But twice within one month his landlady, not hearing his tread on the stairs, had gone round to the club and found him slumped on the floor of the lounge: he had fainted while setting the furniture back in place. She had written to his daughter, and his daughter and her husband had persuaded him to give up his job and his room and come down to them. "Join the fun," his son-in-law had written.

The fainting spells had frightened him, so although he was set in his ways, he had welcomed his daughter's invitation. He suddenly didn't want to live alone any longer. Sundays he used always to visit friends, the Hermanns—who ran a combination zoo and restaurant on the highway just outside of town—but they were the nearest to family he had in that town. It would be nice, he'd thought, to be a family man again. He had seen little of his daughter since she was thirteen. After his wife's death she had gone to live with an aunt. But he remembered an obedient child, coming to him with her homework —listening quietly as he talked, nodding her head forward slightly, as though to take the yoke; a big robust but soft girl, like her mother. To his surprise, he found himself weeping suddenly about his wife's long-ago death. Mrs. Hermann told him, "It's time you met your grand-children. And it's time you had a little fuss made over you. You'll enjoy yourself. It must be like the Garden of Eden down there." His son-in-law ran a string of tourist cabins and Jack Hanna thought that he could keep busy enough: he would be able to show the boy a lot about how to make the grounds more attractive.

A friend of his son-in-law's had been driving down and it was arranged for Hanna to drive with him. He looked forward to the sights along the way, but his son-in-law's friend liked to make time. Hanna told his daughter, "It was just a blur. It hurt my eyes to look out." However, the second morning of the trip, when he stepped out of the door of their motel, he found a grapefruit tree growing in the yard. He spoke of this to his daughter three times, the day he arrived. "Yes indeed! The grapefruit hanging right there, in front of my eyes!" For some reason the grapefruit tree seemed really to promise the pleasanter life Mrs. Hermann was sure of for him.

But very soon it was plain to him that he'd made a mistake in coming. In the first place, Ed didn't need his advice. He was perfectly nice to him and willingly gave him house space, but any time Hanna offered a suggestion he answered cheerfully, "Ah, you're here to take it easy now, Pop." Ed didn't feel that his property needed any land-scaping. "You don't need to plant anything in this state," he said, "Stuff just grows up by itself." His daughter, Ellen, was a dutiful girl still; but it was to her husband now that she resolutely bowed her head. The first week down there, Hanna had said, "I tell you what you ought to have around the cottages." "Oh, Ed does all that," she'd said, before he could get his idea out. Any time her father offered advice, an instant dent was printed upon her brow, a little pucker of loyalty to Ed. "I could build you some shelves there," he'd say. "Oh, Ed likes to do that kind of thing," she'd answer hastily. He found there was nothing at all for him to do; he was an extraneous member of the household. The children would sometimes assign him work: "Grandpa will do my pigtails," "Grandpa will button me up." But his daughter was too conscientious to allow this. "He doesn't know how. That's what a mama is for." Or if he'd try to run the vacuum for her, or clear up the dishes, "No, no!" she'd cry. "It's my job! You're our guest!"—a look on her face as though he were trying to wrest something from her.

So he was without occupation suddenly, and without authority. He felt derelict. The children made him feel it even more so. They hadn't been brought up in the old-fashioned manner, like the Hermann children. They tried to order him out of his chair. They liked

to unlace his shoes, playing at shoe-store. They liked to get all his clothes out of the closet and dress up in them. It gave him an uncomfortable feeling to see his jackets and his neckties and his shoes walking about on them. "I'm not just pickings yet," he told his daughter—who was hurt by his attitude. He felt affection for them involuntarily. This affection took him by surprise sometimes; he was touched by the family resemblance in their faces. But he found he couldn't stay in the house with them.

He began to spend his days down by the fishing wharf. He bought himself a fishing rod and for a few days he tried to pretend to himself that he was busy fishing. But after a while he had taken to sitting there with his eyes shut.

At first, he had gone on long walks. He'd walk out toward the main highway, looking over the little settlement here; or he'd walk along the beach. But he disliked the straggling village. He had always had a passion for neatness. This place had an improvised look—the fishermen's cottages and tourist accommodations scattered about in as haphazard a fashion as the flocks of heron he sometimes saw settled like laundry in the nearby brush to take the sun; then, startled at his approach, flapping away. He missed tidy lawns and shrubbery; he missed fences. The buildings all looked flimsy. At first he marvelled at the palms and the mangrove and the various extraordinary blooms to be seen, but after a little, this began to depress him too. As Ed said, no trick was needed to make things grow. He was irrelevant. He grew quickly, too, to hate his walks along the beach. He disliked the incessant whispering of the sea—never for a syllable silent; and he disliked its incessant casting up of shells, of skeletons, of weeds—each day a different discharge of them. Everything was mumbled by the waves into a form different from itself. He picked up a bright blue fossil, a bit of lava-like stone. He brought it home to ask what it could be. The oldest child knew at once: bubble gum. He threw it quickly into his wastepaper basket. It bothered him that he couldn't always recognise a spot where he'd been the day before. He'd take his bearings by a piece of driftwood or a particular drift of sand. The next day, it would be gone. When he looked out at the horizon, it awoke in him an awe that was unpleasant—especially at those hours when sea and sky blend. He found the thought of death occurring to him. He stopped walking on the beach and began instead to sit out the day down by the wharf.

He had made one friend—Floy, a young fisherman who sometimes dropped in at the house: a big soft-limbed fellow with a dissatisfied look and a ruddy complexion that enthusiasm could shine up quickly, like an apple. He was the only one of Ed's friends who took any particular notice of Hanna when he was there, and troubled to speak a few words to him. For others, the old man was just one chair in which they didn't sit down. Floy sometimes stopped on the wharf to talk with him, too. They had in common their distaste for this part of the world. Jack Hanna liked to listen to Floy on the subject.

"That's it, that's it," he'd nod and nod, with a zest suddenly, with spite; "Damned fools both of us, to be here!"

Floy was from Alabama and always talked of returning. He never had liked fish, he'd complain, or the sea. What he really wanted to do was to farm. What he *really* wanted to do—now his face would shine up for a moment—was run a combination farm and restaurant, everything on the menu grown right there.

"That's an idea," Hanna encouraged him. He had a friend who ran a combination restaurant and zoo. Different idea, of course. He, Hanna, had grown things too, once. He told Floy all about himself.

"On a farm," Floy would take it up again, "there they sit, the rows you've planted—just where you put them." He'd begin to complain again: "Did you know fish never sleep? Some of them never even stand still. If they stand still, something goes wrong. Their metabolism. They sicken."

"Terrible," Hanna would agree. "Damned fools, both of us!" It was some relief to say it.

Hanna didn't get to see very much of Floy, however. Floy was popular with the girls. This was perhaps the reason why he never got back to Alabama. The girls down there on vacation would flirt with him for a while and then be off North again. Some girl was always saying goodbye to him. He'd look after her wistfully and decide to become a farmer. But then there would be another girl along. Jack Hanna was left, for the most part, to himself.

He sat on the sea wall, his fishing rod stuck out before him, his feet dangling above the water, feeling useless; feeling sometimes angry about it, but more often now listless. He sat there day after day. What he caught he gave to Floy for bait. His catch was seldom larger. There were always a few others there fishing—tourist ladies, village boys, another old man like himself, whom he avoided and who avoided him—out of some instinct, both, that they would depress each other further. There was a coming and going, all day, to and from the many small boats tied up at the dock—fishing boats and pleasure boats knocking together in the tide. Hanna no longer observed all this activity. His eyes shut, he sat remembering in slow sleepy snatches scenes out of the life from which he had been uprooted. He remembered now a scolding he'd given some boys for playing hide-and-seek among his rhododendron; another he'd delivered to one of the club members, for picking himself a bouquet of marigold. "Couldn't resist them, Hanna. You shouldn't grow such pretty flowers." He interrupted his own thoughts, yawning. He had prolonged fits of yawning these days. He should write to the Hermanns, he thought. He'd had a letter from the youngest child last week. "Catch me an alligator," the boy had asked. He hadn't written to them in many days. What was there to put into a letter? He sat, then, not even alive to memories; sat merely feeling uncomfortable, sat wishing that his socks were not full of sand, that the sunlight did not strike so fiercely from the restless water.

His hands jerked out in front of him. Something was caught on his line and violently convulsed it. He yanked the pole up, he scrambled to his feet, and swung his catch gingerly to land. A snake writhed from the hook. The barb was caught in its jaw and, wriggling, it was tangling itself in the line.

A young man in swimming trunks hurried over: "Hey, you caught yourself a sea serpent!"

An aged fisherman, who'd just brought in his boat, stepped up to them: "Better throw that fish back, mister. He's a rattle snake."

"He's a rattle snake," Hanna echoed vaguely.

"Wow," said the bather.

Hanna stared at the snake in disgust, holding the pole tightly with both hands, and out at arm's length from him. He blinked about him with irritation, like a man just roused from a nap.

Two young women—friends of Floy—came running up to see. Hanna looked about for Floy but didn't see him. "Oo, oo!" said the girls, "we've been swimming in that water!"

"He's a rattler," the young man in swimming trunks told them briskly. "Don't get too close."

Hanna gave his head a shake and suddenly felt awake. "Yes!" he declared, "a rattler! I have a friend up North would like to have this snake. Friend with a zoo," he informed the others. "Yes indeed!" He lifted the fishing pole a tiny bit and gave it a wiggle. The snake performed undulations. The bystanders stepped back. Hanna laughed. "Ha. Asked me to get him an alligator. But guess this will do."

The bather suggested, "Don't wave him around."

"I've got him all right, don't worry," said Hanna.

The second old man shuffled up and stared. "How'd you get him on there?"

"Just—snagged him," said Hanna, feeling efficient.

Two young boys joined the circle round him. He gave them a sharp look. "You boys keep your distance," he advised, and his voice had again its ancient authority.

"Now I need a box to ship this snake in," he declared. He fastened his eye on the fisherman. "Do you think you could pack him in a box for me?"

The fisherman shrugged his shoulders lightly. "Can't help you there."

Hanna turned to the young man in swimming trunks.

"Sorry, Pop, but I never touch them," said the young man, glancing toward the two young women, who giggled.

Hanna gave him a look of stern annoyance. Then he glared at the snake. The snake, from out its cats-cradle tangle, darted its flat head here and there.

"The shell shop," Hanna decided. He'd seen their sign in the window: "We mail anywhere. Send your friends a souvenir shell collection." And a sample box. The box had been the right size. He started off, dangling his snake from the pole. The others followed at a little distance. The shell shop was just around the corner.

As he led the way, Hanna framed in his mind the letter he

would send the Hermanns. "Dear friends, You will see that I have not been idle." He gave his snake the gentlest flick in the air. It hissed. He laughed, and for a moment as his feet moved neatly along the road, he felt as if he danced.

A bell rang when the screen door of the shell shop opened. The two elderly ladies who ran the shop looked round. Both of them backed up against the counter. Hanna began, "Ladies, don't be nervous. I have a souvenir—" But they interrupted him: "Take it out! Out!" Hanna backed out the door again.

On the street, he avoided glancing at his audience. The little crowd awaited his next move silently. He gazed right and left, up and down the village road. "Best place to go is straight to the post office, I guess," he said at last. "Wonder if I should put in something for him to eat. What do you suppose he eats?"

"Airline hostesses," said the bather.

Hanna ignored this answer. No one else spoke up. "Guess he's all right for the trip," Hanna decided. "My friend will feed him at the other end." He hoisted the snake.

Inside the post office, a dozen people were lined up to ask for their mail. As Hanna stepped in, they scattered.

"Have you got somebody back there who would wrap this snake for me?" he called out cheerfully.

The postmistress stuck her head out the window. "No sirree," she told him.

He explained about his friend up North.

She told him, "Come on, Pop, get him out of here. There's a heavy mail today."

Not many people took their places again in line. When Hanna emerged from the post office, his audience was twice its former size. It was a quiet crowd. The sight of a snake hushed people down. Everybody stood about without a word, just waiting to see what Hanna would do.

Hanna lowered the snake again to the ground. Tired of wriggling, it lay there in the hot sun, sluggish, confused. It stuck out its tongue. But when a young man in a flapping sports shirt stepped close suddenly, it gathered itself together and rattled. At the sound, Hanna's enthusiasm revived. He scanned the crowd with a bold eye. "I need somebody to put this snake in a box for me," he declared.

Just then Floy came round the corner. "Here's the man," said Hanna.

The two girls who knew Floy started chattering at him at once: "You might have *told* us there were snakes in that bay! We've been in and out of that water, you know!"

Floy, rubbing his chin, stared at the rattle snake. "Well," he said, "you're quite a fisherman after all."

Hanna smiled at the crowd. He felt more leisurely now. He said, "I didn't know snakes went swimming."

Floy told him, "I know a man was out deep-sea fishing, a hundred miles from shore, and saw one swimming along."

"Where was he swimming to?" the girls cried. "A hundred miles out! Imagine!"

"Lord knows," said Floy. "Figured to himself it was somewhere, I suppose." He winked at Hanna. "We all keep hoping. Well," he asked, "What do you aim to do with him, Jack?"

The crowd made way. The town sheriff strode up—a short thickset man, heavy-hipped. Hanna stood aside, to let the sheriff see what he had, and his eyes were glittering like a boy's. He told Floy, "My friend up North with the zoo will appreciate receiving it. I've been looking for the man to pack him in a box for me."

The sheriff said, "I'll pack him up for you." He pulled his pistol from its holster and shot the snake—twice—through the head. Then, as the crowd murmured, he took out a big handkerchief and wiped his pistol and put it back in its holster. The snake twitched and lay slack. A small spotted dog appeared out of nowhere to lick up its blood. Pleased with himself, the sheriff puffed out his chest.

Jack Hanna stood there with his mouth open. He flushed violently and his lower lip began to tremble.

Floy looked at him with surprise and looked away. He told the sheriff, "That was a mean thing to do. You might at least have given him some warning."

The sheriff stared at him. "My job is to protect the citizenry," he said. With a hurt look, his hand on his holster, he strode off. The crowd dispersed.

"Hey," Floy said to Hanna, "I'll get you the rattles." He took out his knife and, crouching down, sawed at the snake's tail. "Here," he said, getting up, "Hold them carefully. They're alive, you know, for seven hours after."

Hanna held out his hand and Floy set the rattles in it. "Can you feel it?" Hanna squinted at the rattles and nodded vaguely.

Then he looked up at Floy, as if for further instructions. But one of the girls called back to Floy, "Aren't you coming, you slow old thing?" Floy shrugged, smiled at Hanna, apologetic, and joined the girls.

Hanna walked off by himself, holding the rattles carefully in his hand. He took Floy's word for fact, and felt a little thrill of fascination at the thought that this remnant could still have life in it. But he wasn't sure what good that was.

from A Book of Travail

Although it is you who have sent me away, it is to you that I address this book—a book of travels. (Spell that as you wish.) You do not wait for me to return. You weave, unweave, in my absence, no images of a future in which our figures are joined. Nevertheless it is you I go seeking. That makes me perhaps mad. And yet, as I cast myself upon countries strange to me, God grant me only this: that I do not forget you.

My words come very strangely. I have been talking every language but my own. (And had I ever learned *that* well? At any rate, it never served me to persuade you that you loved me.) And now my words are a little mixed with dust and with salt, as I try to speak. I can see you frowning, trying to make them out—your eyes very yellow-black, regarding me boldly. It is not possible to love you lightly. I love you or I love you not. So I will be bold, too, and whether or not I know how, speak.

Where should I begin? Begin anywhere, you would say. Let me begin with a tale that may shock you. Not that that is my pleasure. I went seeking you.

I had been gone two weeks. Your first letter had been in Athens to meet me—to speak a welcome and to speak regret. (It would be nice if heart *could* answer heart as face answers face in water.) In the meantime two letters from me would have reached you, and might have cut you from me altogether (I spoke presumptuously), or might at last, by a miracle, have stirred in you love. That is the letter I waited for: "I find that I love you." I went travelling after those words over miles and miles. You will read this in bewilderment. For hadn't I declared to you that I accepted your words—that you did *not* love me? I meant what I said with all my heart. I could read in your every motion the distress my hopes caused you. So how could I do otherwise than disarm myself before you—lay down all hopes? And yet, speaking this, and meaning this, I continued to hope all things. Love

is not reasonable. Is it not, perhaps, even necessary that this be so—
that, throwing down every weapon it knows, stripped to nothing, it
should still continue simply to stand before the city it longs to take,
the loved walls, waiting for them to fall.

No further letter from you had come, and I left Athens for one
of the islands. Take ship, I felt, take ship, and as the world is round,
you may reach home again. For this is how I had sailed away from
you.

The airs above the sea are full of echoes, colliding. I had spoken
my love, I had taken my leave, I had set off. The ship headed out into
the wind. That wind circled my head, whirled round my ears, all my
own words again. Here was a young man, eyes large, leaning toward
me, saying: "Your life is more real to me than my own life. I feel so
confident that I could make you happy. It is unbearable to me that I
shouldn't be allowed to try." Yes, it was Russell. You had given me a
letter to him; and he had hardly put the letter down, to smile at me
again, before he was in love with me. This will not surprise you.
Because he is young, and a poet, and must fall in love as others must
eat, or grow faint. So young that he took no heed of where his words
might blow. The wind might carry them round and about the boat
and to where his wife was sitting—whom he would not want to harm.
He loved her too, of course. Better than he knew or she knew. But the
world was so immense. I could see his eyes glinting across the waters
as the ship moved out over them, his glance nervous. "It's as though I
let life go by me," he was saying. "Mustn't one catch at it, mustn't one
fling oneself after it?" One can't fling oneself in all directions, I was
trying to say. But he burned to. I think he would have liked to have
flung himself, in sparks, throughout the universe—one spark of him
toward the sun, one toward the moon, one toward each star, and on
earth too, toward every fire. "I love Lisa of course," he was explaining.
"I love her very much. But sometimes when we are walking down the
street together I have to find some excuse to drop behind, I have to
walk at least a few steps behind her, or I can't breathe. I couldn't

imagine ever leaving her. And yet I never can let myself think that I shall be married to her all my life." And he swung his eyes, distractedly, as if to see that far.

There were four of us making that trip together. Lisa you never met. An open-hearted girl, whose eyes followed Russell as if he were the sun in its course, and that course an amazement to her again each day. She wore that look of one taken again and again by surprise— eyes ashine, mouth half open. And she was ready to go wherever surprise might lead her (as long as it were with Russell). And there was with them a young girl, an acquaintance of theirs just arrived from Paris—crop-haired, saucer-eyed, a touch of the tomboy to her— making what giro I did not know, but it was somewhere she wanted to get, though I think perhaps she didn't know, either, where that was. She was dressed for the road, in strange, rather charming mixed garb: sneakers, socks, a striped skirt, a plaid shirt, with a worker's bandana at her throat and on her head a funny little round cotton hat, a canteen over her shoulder, and her guide book swung on a strap—Kit. She talked of someone back in Athens whom she was trying to persuade to go with her to Crete. But this person could never set a date, and she had only so much time before she must return to Paris, to vague studies there. She talked a little tough—gay knowing talk. But her very blue eyes were a child's. There was also on board an English girl, who when she had spotted us among the Greeks had moved in our direction, shy, almost prim, hardly venturing to speak, but placing herself near us. Lisa had soon won her to speech, and as night fell we shared together our assortments of food. We had oranges, cheese and, from Kit's canteen, wine. She contributed chocolate and tea biscuits.

We were travelling as deck passengers. But Russell had come off that morning forgetting the blankets he was to carry. Nor had the English girl any cover with her. I had an old brown quilt and we spread it out to see how many might creep under. Four of us could, the four girls. The bit of deck we'd chosen was not sheltered, and the wind kept lifting the edges of the quilt, rippling it over us like a stage-set sea. A Greek rose from a spot more mid-ship and beckoned that we must take his place—and simply walked away, that there might be no argument. For that is how these people are with strangers. We moved in among a circle of sleepers. Kit looked cold still, was trying to make the edges of the quilt tuck under us. A Greek woman turned back the striped rug in which she lay wrapped and gestured for Kit to come in with her, and, when she hesitated, spoke to her, in the strange language, peremptorily, humorously; so Kit accepted the hospitality. "Ah, it's warm as a furnace here," she called to us in a little girl's voice. At the rail, the man who had moved for us joined Russell: "We don't have to sleep." Russell grinned, but the look he turned toward us then, through the dusk, was a frail one, forlorn. So some of us dozed. Over us the stars swung as though on cords. And from the rail Russell glanced our way, or out to sea—his gaze wandered beyond the arc of huddled sleepers and huddled creatures, the goats, the chickens, legs tied under them, uttering their quavery cries (the goats, their chins on the deck, eyes flicking, the chickens, heads buried in feathers, but raising them now and then, as on a stick, to complain). Toward midnight, waking, I could see Russell walking up and down flailing his arms. The other man had vanished. At the rail some leaning sailors wailed an ancient, a harsh tune—emptying their throats of it; then flung themselves to the deck and sprawled in attitudes of death. The stars were too close and the sea was too close. I waved my hand at Russell, and he peered across at me like a new-born soul, like a child set adrift on a stream and waiting the hand that will pluck it forth.

Before dawn, islands drew near: a speckle of thin lights, a port,

the delicate lights—pink yellow pink blue—making the water smile. We dropped anchor, out from land. And at our side small boats, appearing, tossed like paper, the crews clinging to us with their hands, one rope tossed, and up the flimsy ship's ladder three men clambering, one, a cripple, dragged by the others, thump thump up each step, grimacing but unalarmed; then down the ladder disembarked a disordered (but unalarmed) small crowd, men babies women rugs baskets a green trunk a violin three chickens flapping upside down—and we moved off again, the pale lights vanishing. And we had dreamed it, delicately.

Then at dawn we woke again, rubbing our eyes, and Mykonos shone there. And this time we went in, in one of the crowded small boats, toward the line along the shore of waiting Greeks—the welcoming line shaped there at any hour. The boats moved in quietly (though one old Greek woman in our boat was laughing gigantically at something). Russell looked pale, looked very slight of frame. The English girl, gripping her small satchel, sat crouched forward, staring toward land, her eyes glazed, her face, in the dawning, full of alarm, full of dreams. The boat rocked and her glance met mine, but her face did not change, she was so tranced. Then suddenly she recognised, in the line along the shore, friends, the couple she was visiting, and woke out of that sleep, and began to wave, giggling, conscious again.

Our shipload was scattered. The four of us headed for the house where we had rooms—a house where Russell and Lisa had stayed the summer before (earning their keep on the island by giving English lessons). And here we curled up again, and dozed, until light was full. Then we rose and all day walked that white island. Russell had revived, and as we walked he put questions to me. "What do you think is the condition of modern poetry?" "Don't you believe, then, that it's the poet's duty to find a language in which he can communicate with all men of his time?" "Do you believe in God?" "Why do you believe in God?" "Ah, Russell," Lisa would cry, "look, look—how pink the sea is there!" "Look, look at the flowers on that slope!" "Look," she

would cry, "look—do you remember the day we stopped at that house?"

I wanted to say to her: "You need not fear me. If you knew how violently my thoughts flew elsewhere." But I didn't know how to say this. Kit meanwhile wanted Lisa to teach her Greek songs, and they walked echoing: *"Su-pa ma-ma—su-pa ma-ma*—Mother find me a husband. And I do not want an old man." Russell didn't know what he did. I was a book he wanted to read. He was a book he wanted *me* to read. He stepped beside me, swinging his hands as if he danced— gesticulating, frowning, sought my eye. And his eye said: If I ask for bread, will you give me a stone?

But I found it hard to reply to his catechism. This island we walked—. Rock. A piece of rock set in the sea. But from this rock light strikes sparks, sparks into flowers. Light struck, here it was that I began to believe: if you would only come (you had spoken of a visit as possible)—if you would only come—surely—this light might strike from your breast love. And so I went dreaming.

At the sea we had our lunch. Retsina from Kit's canteen. Olives. Cheese. The bread had been forgotten. It didn't matter. Ill-assorted as we were, joining hands, we attempted a Greek dance, witless, danced into the sea, having to hop out in disorder. We walked a long way home then, a rocky up-and-down-winding shepherd's path, picking the million small blazing flowers as we went, so weary soon that we staggered; and Kit actually stumbled and fell, angry at herself, the canteen flung from her shoulder. At the top of one hill, our tongues out, we agreed to beg some water. A peasant's house was set there, high above the sea. The man came out at our calling and fetched us the water, in a large tumbler, emptying and refilling, with ceremony, for each—his pig, his chickens, and his goat regarding us mildly. Revived, we thanked him mightily; and he stared at us, in the eye, out of his ugly pleasant face, and "It's not such a very great thing," he said, "to give you a drink of water." And we limped off again, down toward the shining whitewashed town.

We ate that night at a tavern on the waterfront, a barnlike room opening onto beach and ships—a crowded mishmosh of tables, brown faces gathered. At our entrance there were shouts, arms raised. Russell and Lisa moved eagerly among the tables, renewing friendships. A couple of musicians were flaring away—a violinist, a guitarist. Close as we could to their vibration, we found room at a table. Two men were seated there before us, friends it seemed, but one very different from the other; one was plainly of this island, the other—well, at the other I barely looked, for I was looking at the man across from me. He sat over a great plate of fish, the crisscross bones scattered to the table, and his glass spilling wine. The table top swam. As we sat, he lifted the decanter and splashed our glasses full. The custom here is that one fills a glass only halfway to the top. Not to be uncongenial but the reverse, for this makes it necessary to dip decanter toward glass more frequently. But this man could not possibly stay his hand half-way; the glass must run over. But he could keep the decanter in motion, too, for he would pour again whether or not the necessity had arrived. Russell knew this man and introduced him: Cyclops. Yes, he had one eye—the other lost, not as one began imagining, in some festive act of recklessness, but as the result of a childhood illness. The one eye, very blue, set shining in a long face, set in leather; the other eye out but the blind socket gesticulating still, out of that gone eye tears dropping often, not for grief; the cheek wrinkling, the brow above it lifting, and the tears brimming as the wine

brimmed at his hand, out of extravagance of spirit.

"Your health," Kit toasted, suddenly lively.

"We'll arrange for that," he cried—Russell translating. And stared at her with a wise look, which both devoured her and did without; and jerked his head back and laughed; and the tears sprang from his dead eye.

"He is a fisherman," the man at my left announced. "A bachelor fisherman. And a King." And he turned to me. "He is a King."

The King got up to dance. The musicians had begun a new tune and he pushed back his chair and stepped into the small dancing space somehow managed here among all the tables. He was a long, bony man, dressed in very worn britches, a layer of raggedy shirts, a bulky gray cummerbund wrapping it all together, barefoot. He began to strike the boards with his feet—light, then hard—and move, foot crossing foot, in circles, eyes down, watching the ground he danced, hands hitching up his trousers at the groin, then clapping the air, then, as he bent his knee, clapping the ground.

The other man joined him, laughing. This man was dressed in a double-breasted gray city suit, full in cut. A medium sized man, and pleasant enough in looks, but a little plump-chested, a little soft. I remember I felt for him at that first meeting a slight spontaneous distaste. He echoed Cyclop's motions now in a dance of his own, the steps the same yet not the same, a subtle difference intruding. He had been to America, one gathered. He just perceptibly swung the dance. But I still do know how to dance it, his motions also proclaimed, self consciously.

When he came back to the table, he wanted to talk. Cyclops had tipped back his head and begun to sing, and it was hard to listen to any other. But I did half listen, and he sat there telling about himself with a peculiar urgency. He was telling me that, yes, he had been in America. He had spent two, three years there at a certain hospital. I muttered words of commiseration, but hadn't heard him right: he hadn't been ill, but was a doctor, and had studied in America, now had returned to his own country to practise.

Most of what he said I lost. Weariness had made me deaf. The evening spun round me and blurred, faces and voices mixed, only one image holding an outline: Cyclops spilling song with wine, his head back, mouth opening as if to yawn, gone eye gesticulating: *"Asemay, Asemay*—Let me live alone, let me forget you!"—a joyous baying. The four of us staggered the ghostly streets home.

The next day again we walked the island, this time taking the opposite direction, the sea on our left (striped violet, electric); walked again to a far beach. Flowers burned the ground and bees the air. The day flung light so wide that the far looked near as the near. We wandered until the day was out; then headed for the doctor's. For the doctor had found us that morning, as we took our coffee on the waterfront, and had sat again to talk, and had ended by asking us for dinner.

His house was set at the edge of town, and half way up the slope the town climbed from the sea. A raised terrace circled it. One mounted by steps from the street. The doctor was out here, staring down into the town. But the door open behind him rayed light and voices. The other guests were gathered, and the banquet spread.

The other guests were Cyclops and the two musicians. The banquet—was that. The table held lobster, fish, chicken, rice, squash, cheese. The edge of one platter rested upon that of the next. All this had been prepared by the girl who kept his house ("She is only a child," said the doctor—"a miller's daughter"), and who moved now, as we sat, to set before us still further dishes. A small brother kept her company in the kitchen; stood now in the doorway, lightly on one foot, to watch the plates go round.

The doctor stood to carve the lobster; the violinist to carve the chicken; the guitarist to spear out fish. Each vied to see his neighbor's plate heaped higher than his own. Cyclops stood to splash the glasses full. Their moving arms tangled, a festive vine.

In the passing, Cyclops' plate vanished somewhere—into the

kitchen perhaps, for some repair. Kit, at Cyclops' side, expressed distress, the doctor translating.

But "You eat, and I am satisfied," he cried.

Sun had flushed us all, this day, but Kit flushed pinker now, and blinked, her eyes rounding—a bigger, a more startled blue, it seemed, each moment.

The doctor wanted to tell us about Cyclops. "He is a fisherman, but he is a King," he announced, as he had the evening before. "He lives with his mother. He goes out and catches as much fish as he needs to keep house for himself and his mother. And no more. When she tells him he's lazy, 'Did I bring you home dinner tonight?' he asks her. His bed is right by the door, so that when he comes home full of wine, he doesn't need to look for it; he can fall down and be in bed. He fishes for his living. When he has his living, he stops. Then he is a leisured man. He is royalty. He walks about and he enjoys the world around him. He sits in the sun. He opens his mouth and sings. He pours wine down his throat." The doctor, talking, rose and wound the gramophone. A tavern melody began to circle. "This gramophone," the doctor interrupted himself, "belonged to . . ."

The floor gave a sound like a drum. In one barefoot leap, having, it seemed, not even to push back his chair, Cyclops had left the table. Arms spread like wings, he twirled around the room, a great barefoot bird, stepping, leaping, hands clapping the air, with a hush, the ground. With one final floor-thudding somersault, he rejoined us. The doctor was beaming at us. "I haven't let him drink all day. That's why he is dancing well."

The miller's daughter changed the record. In the doorway now her small brother lightly hinted a dance, his feet in one place, scarcely moving, yet dancing; then catching my eye, smiled rapidly in confusion and ducked away. Cyclops splashed all the glasses full. The doctor wanted to talk. He wanted to talk about Cyclops. He wanted to talk about himself.

"I had thought," he was saying about himself, "that one couldn't choose a life that would be more rewarding—to make people well again. But it isn't so, it isn't so," he was saying. "Everywhere is simply wretchedness." Russell was straining forward, trying to follow. He was biting his lip, straining toward him. But one couldn't quite follow the doctor. Or perhaps we had drunk too much wine. "My friend came into my room one day, at the hospital. 'What do you believe, George?' he asked me. 'Beethoven,' I told him. The day I first heard Beethoven, I wanted to kill myself. Who am I?"

Kit was flirting with Cyclops. She wanted the doctor to translate. He translated. Then he got up to look for his album of Beethoven.

He came back beaming again as a symphony began to shake the small room. Everybody hushed down. Cyclops cocked his head and listened; then without thinking he opened his throat and began to howl his own ancient tune, more familiar refrain: "*Asemay, Asemay*—Let me forget you, let me live alone!" His blind eye sprang great tears. The doctor laughed and poured Cyclops more wine. "He'll be in here tomorrow, though," he told us, "and ask to hear it again."

The lobster vanished, the chicken vanished, the fish vanished. The Beethoven concluded. "Let's dance," said the doctor. The table was pushed back and the plates were carried off into the kitchen. The musicians wiped their hands and brought out their fiddles. Another bottle of wine was found. We had walked this island all one day and the next and we could almost dance, ourselves, Cyclops' dance. He discarded a few shirts now. Arms raised, his foot raised, he again tried the earth. Who is to say, lightly, that it will hold one? He steps out— hush—and again—and kneeling quickly, touches the ground with his hand. Yes, he sets his foot down before him as though it were the day of Creation all over again.

The doctor must dance too. He shed his coat. He shook his leg, put out his arms like chicken wings, then, one hand behind his head —a Greek gesture—flirtatious, kicked off his shoes.

And Russell must dance. He leapt into it, eyes bright. Lisa joined him.

Soon we all danced. The floor thundered. The miller came by for his daughter. And he paused to dance too.

Everybody danced on and on. The doctor danced again until his forehead shone, his shirt clung to him plumply. Cyclops danced, wine in hand, the wine spilling. Danced without thought. His arms, legs danced. The dance danced. The doctor was like a bird trying to fly— but this bird cannot; but cannot stop flapping, running, stretching out all his feathers. He was dancing with his heart in his eyes: Tell me— who am I? Cyclops' great feet struck sparks from the boards. The doctor couldn't help but stare at him. Nor could any of us. He was our delirium, this one-eyed man.

What were we all trying to dance?

It was late when an oldish weary man appeared in the doorway. The doctor, flushed from the dance, turning, still half danced toward the man, slowing to a grave stop before him. They spoke briefly. Then the doctor crossed to me where I was sitting, drink in hand, catching my breath. And "Please, would you like to come with me," he asked. "I have to go to a patient—a boy with tetanus." And he got his jacket. We groped our way from the lightstruck room down the stairs outside into the street, following the weary man.

We followed the man through the dim maze of the town. The doctor took my hand. And I started to withdraw it. But that seemed an ugly motion. So holding hands, as though we were children, we stumbled the uneven night streets. At the waterfront, by a café, he spoke to the other, who nodded and vanished. We sat down at a table out front. The doctor ordered two coffees, black.

He began to talk again. Beyond us shone the sea. The small boats were tipping in it lightly. We were the only ones sitting there. A dog limped by, turning its head to look at us.

"Why don't you stay," the doctor asked, "and be my nurse here? Do you have to go?"

"I have to go," I told him. "I have to go tomorrow."

"You don't have to go," he said. "Stay."

"How old is the child with tetanus?" I asked him.

"He's twelve," he said. "Stay. The day I came back here," the doctor said, "the day I arrived at this island, I stood on the shore, and I looked at the pebbles at my feet, I looked at the boats in the surf, and I started to cry. I had been so homesick—in America. But I'm a stranger after all. And I'm lonely."

"Were you born on this island?" I asked him.

He had been born on another island.

I asked him about his practise.

"I can't really make any difference at all," he said. He leaned toward me with an exhausted look. He wanted to tell me about a call he had had one night. A boy in a motor boat had collided with a larger boat. "His brains were lying on his cheek," he said. "They came and woke me. It was three in the morning. I said I'd be along. I went back to sleep. They came and woke me again. I got out of bed and started to dress. And I lay down and went back to sleep. They came again—."

We glanced up and Russell was standing there. He wanted to come with us. He sat down and ordered a coffee too. The doctor didn't finish his story. Russell began to inquire about the boy with tetanus. He knew the mother slightly. The man who had come to fetch the doctor reappeared. The doctor drained his cup and stood up. "Yes, come with us," he said to Russell.

One mounted to this house, too, by steep outside stairs. The room was the first into which we stepped, a whitewashed dim-shining room. There was little in it but the bed in which the sick boy lay, his limbs flung out under the sheet, around him gathered relatives. Russell stood near, joined that half-circle. He knew some of these people. But I felt incongruous there—though they turned to look at me without reproach. I stayed by the door.

Someone went into the back room for a lantern, so that the doctor could see. The doctor whispered urgently, "Cover the light!" As its blaze whitened the room, the boy's body arched, and he began to moan through his teeth. They shaded the lantern quickly. The doctor turned back the sheet and ran his hands along the boy's anguished limbs.

The boy wanted to speak, but his jaw was locked; and it was as though he had forgotten how to speak, sought again to know what speech was. The doctor covered him again, and sat beside him to prepare the hypodermic needles he must give him. The family, in its gathered arc, watched in silence. One woman covered the boy's eyes with a cloth, and she kept her hand there then, on his head. He had the shaven head of all Greek boys, large domed, and the great widely spaced dark eyes.

The others bent toward him, their hands by their sides, yet touching him, and touching him with their eyes. And one held the shaded light. The bed in its disarray of limbs was queerly beautiful. His body arched and arched again. The doctor put the needle in his arm and held it there. They had all been standing there, one knew, hour after hour, watching him, trying to read from the hieroglyph of his limbs in spasm: Will he live—will he speak, will he walk—will he be born again?

The doctor gave him several needles. He questioned one of the women. Then he stood up. "Wish them good night," he told us. We wished them, in whispers, good night. We descended the dim stairs again.

"Will he live?" Russell asked.

"Yes, he's going to live," the doctor said. "He's lucky."

And we walked back through the town to the doctor's house. The terrace smelled of carnations. Through the windows, music still spilled. The doctor took my hand. Russell stepped in the door, toward the music, but the doctor, with the pressure of his hand, asked me to stay. I stayed. One could hear Cyclops' bare feet stepping the boards inside. And then Russell join the dance. The air was very clear about us, blue, not black. Below us, along the shore, there were bright small flares—night fishing. "I am lonely," the doctor said to me again.

Now this is very strange. He kissed my mouth. And then stood close against me—as though he would vanish, if he could, in my arms. And though I had experienced at first sight for this man distaste, I didn't feel now like drawing away. He led me into the garden to which the terrace circled. Where I began to speak the words I knew one should speak: "I must not." But when he said, "Please don't say that you must not," I stopped speaking. And felt for this man no desire, but something far simpler than desire. And yes I fell down under him. And though I knew no pleasure, yet for those moments the world seemed to lie there intact, hammered together again.

Then he picked a carnation for me. And we stepped back into the room where Cyclops was somersaulting.

And why have I told you this tale?

This book was set on the linotype in Fairfield.
The display type is Bell.
The composition is by H. Wolff Book Manufacturing Co., New York.
The printing is by Noble Offset Printers Inc., New York.
The binding is by H. Wolff Book Manufacturing Co., New York.
Designed by Jacqueline Schuman.